The Meritocrats

The Meritocrats

WILLIAM HAGGARD

HODDER AND STOUGHTON
LONDON SYDNEY AUCKLAND TORONTO

British Library Cataloguing in Publication Data
Haggard, William
  The meritocrats.
  Rn: Richard Henry Michael Clayton   I. Title
  823'.914[F]   PR6058.A37/

ISBN 0 340 36759 8

Prologue

The plane was a spyplane and in no way ashamed of it. It wasn't one of the latest or biggest, not an AWAC with its clumsy dome, but it was big enough for a simple task and that was to find out as surely as possible why an Afghan village had been burnt to the ground. That had happened before with sickening frequency but this fire had been started by bombs from the air, an extravagant piece of overkill if you had merely wanted to murder the villagers, and moreover, before the bombs had fallen, Russian tanks had been driven in and abandoned. All this had come from refugees and it wasn't in the normal pattern. Why drive your own tanks to a target you meant to destroy?

So the spyplane was flying high and steadily, its outsize wings very slightly shivering. It belonged to the state of Pakistan and indeed bore Pakistani markings but another state had provided and paid for it. The pilot was a Pakistani, a man of the great Punjabi clans which continued to rule the country as of right, but the observer was an American, a technician and a very well-trained one.

At this moment he was feeling a little drunk. Not with alcohol which he seldom used but with the spectacle of the sunrise below him. He had seen it from above before, the golden ball climbing out of infinity, and the sight had always clawed his nerves. God must have felt like this when he made the world. Or rather when, having made it, he pulled the switch.

The pilot's voice was clear in his earphones. "There in about six minutes."

"Good."

"Are we under radar?"

"I'll see."

The observer pressed a coloured button on the formidable

console which curved around him. There were most kinds of electronic gadget. "Negative," he said. He meant "No."

"Can you get what you want from this height?"

"Perhaps."

"But you'd rather have something from lower?"

"Of course."

"Then I think we'll risk going down and getting it. But anything more than small-arms fire and I'm up again like a rocketing pheasant."

They began to spiral down in wide curves. There was smoke from the village still but no flame. In what had been the little square men were loading two tanks onto tank transporters.

The pilot said: "Odd."

"Very odd indeed."

"Have you got what you want?"

"Yes thanks."

"Then let's go."

They turned and began to climb steeply again. The pilot said: "I'm hungry."

"So am I."

"Breakfast for you will be eggs and bacon. I'll have the same but without the bacon. Not that I'm considered orthodox but bacon here has a certain tapeworm."

"Mine will come from a tin."

"And therefore taste horrible."

Both of them were relaxing deliberately and the American asked: "Why weren't we shot at?"

"Why should we be shot at, or rather why here? Probably there was nothing to shoot with. The Russians wanted those tanks back, that's for sure, but there was nothing in a burnt-out village worth defending with ack-ack or missiles. They keep that sort of stuff elsewhere. Such as where we're heading. Just check again if they've got us on radar."

The observer did so and this time said: "Positive."

"Hell."

"What are you going to do?"

"What the book says. Which is to climb to maximum altitude and fly on. Have you baled out before?"

"Only in practice."

"I've been out once because I had to. Bloody Indians in Kashmir, it was." A pause. "Got your cameras unshipped in case you have to jump?"

"If I got home without them I'd be in serious trouble."

"You may have trouble just getting home. It's three hundred miles to a friendly border and the country's pretty rugged between it."

"I do have a survival kit."

"Ever used it for real?"

"I can't say I have."

"Then the god of Christian soldiers go with you. To a modern missile we're sitting ducks. Even if we saw it coming I couldn't take evasive action. This thing would break up in the air if I did that."

"We've been radar-ed before and nothing has happened."

"Maybe we hadn't been over what mattered. I've a hunch that village was highly sensitive."

"Then what do we do?"

"Drone on and hope for the best. It isn't worth trying to divert. They can hold us."

One of the observer's nightmares was the vision of a missile hitting, the crack, the ball of fire, the aircraft disintegrating as it fell like a well-taken bird. But when the strike came it was almost casual, a bump which threw him against his belt, then the sight of the port engine burning.

The Punjabi said: "Proximity fuse, I'd bet my balls. They've got stuff that's a lot more modern than that."

"What are you going to do?"

"Fly on. I've cut that engine. The fire may blow out. *May*, I say. It just sometimes happens."

They flew on for perhaps a minute more. "It's not blowing out, it's spreading fast. When the wing-tank blows we'll go down like a stone. Are you navigating still?"

"Of course."

"Then how far from the frontier?"

"Maybe a hundred."

"I think you'd better jump."

"I'll stay with you."

The pilot swore in broad Punjabi, then switched to a more elegant Urdu. Finally he returned to English. "I'm the

7

captain of this crate. I say Go. Make sure you've got your cameras. Make sure you've got that stupid survival kit."

"And you?"

"I'll fly on."

"I think you're mad."

The pilot said with a simple dignity: "I'm not dotty but I signed a contract. I accepted a very generous salary and one of its terms was No Surrender – no surrender of what this damned thing carries. Some of that stuff of yours is Top Secret. While's there's an outside chance of getting it home I promised that I'd take that chance. But more likely they'll put a new model up and that will blow your junk to pieces."

"With you sitting on it."

"I've eaten your salt and that's important. Now stop arguing and eject as I tell you. Don't take your mask off before it's safe to. Good luck."

"The same to you."

The American pressed the button and went clear. There was a moment of appalling terror till the main chute opened and dragged at his harness. The spyplane could reach an enormous altitude but it wasn't fast since it didn't need to be. The observer could still see it bumbling on, a black outline against the cerulean sky.

Then suddenly it wasn't there and the nightmare was a shocking reality. At that distance he could hear no sound but the ball of flame was compact and deadly. For a moment it hung in the air like a firework, then it fell apart in a shower of debris.

There wouldn't be anything left worth finding.

I

In a room a long way from a spyplane's wreckage two men were making an urgent decision. They were very well equipped to do so since they didn't have to think of elections. National policy was decided for them and both were well content with that but provided they kept within the guidelines, which both had been rigorously trained to do, they could make the day-to-day decisions without fear of any political backlash.

The junior put a report on the table and the senior picked it up and read it. It didn't take him long since the paper was short. It was headed *Tests in Afghanistan*.

The senior asked: "So another failure?"

"The heat was a little higher than last time but nothing like what the British are getting with their ANNE. We monitored their tests at sea."

"And the word has come down that we've got to have it. I quite see that, though I was never a soldier. So long as a NATO power holds ANNE over us our superiority in conventional weapons is something which is balanced, maybe gone. Naturally that upsets the Brass and the Brass has been making my life a misery." The senior poured some tea from a samovar. "This man whom Azimev snared at Yeldham –?"

"Has been sending us pretty high class stuff."

"The scientists don't suspect it's phony?"

"Not yet – why should they? After all they've had some results, they've advanced, and this ANNE is known to be tricky in the extreme. A half of the British tests failed miserably."

"But the other half didn't. A few seconds of heat at God-knows-what-Celsius. A total answer to armour *en masse*. No wonder the Brass is upset. I would be."

9

"Then what do you suggest we do?"

The senior looked at the paper again. "This man of Azimev's at Yeldham – Harrison. How senior is he?"

"Pretty close to the top."

"He would know what there is to be known?"

The junior thought some time before answering; finally he said carefully: "It is known that work has failed at Yeldham too."

"As has ours."

"But not entirely. We've got something far better than napalm or phosphorus and we've got it largely from what Miles Harrison sent us."

It was the senior's turn to think and he did so. "You are suggesting we go on squeezing this Harrison?"

"I am suggesting we give him a little more time. Azimev must make that clear to him. Another report and this time a better one. Our scientists will work on it. If they succeed then we have succeeded. The strategic advantage on land is restored and the brass can think up some new adventure."

"You see no alternative?"

"No. Do you?"

The senior rose and poured more tea; he drank some of it and then said formally: "You may authorise Azimev to proceed as you suggest. He may use all the pressure he dares."

"He will."

"His own career is at stake."

"He will know it."

As the junior was leaving the room the senior unexpectedly stopped him. "So the British call this dreadful thing ANNE?"

"The British have their own sense of humour."

"Whatever they call it it's wholly horrible."

The junior was astonished but hid it. The remark was close to a moral judgement and coming from a senior official was as surprising as a talking ass. ANNE was simply another weapon, one which an enemy had and Russia had not. The situation was as simple as that and a moral judgement smelt strongly of heresy. But he couldn't walk away without answering.

"I suppose it's a matter of personal taste. For myself I'd rather be burnt in a second than die miserably of radiation."

In another room neither round nor square two other men sat, for a moment in silence. One had a very fine head of hair which his enemies put it about was dyed. He was sensitive on the point, denying it, and his barber had been put on telly, insisting to an indifferent world that there was no dye. The other man was a little younger and wore one of those fashionable close-cut grey wigs which made a man look mature but still virile. On the table between them was a formidable file. It was open at an excellent photograph.

Hair tapped it and said: "We must give him a medal."

"I leave you to draft the citation, then."

Hair saw that he'd dropped yet another clanger, for the men of Wig's powerful organisation could neither expect a medal nor get one. Hair covered the slip with his famous smile, the urchin face creasing in lines of false bonhomie. "Then some generous recognition of your own kind."

"That I have already arranged since he put up a fine show and deserves it. He'd sprained an ankle landing badly and when those refugees found him he'd finished his water. They tied him to a mule and brought him in."

"That was a bit of luck."

"No doubt. Good men are inclined to attract good luck."

"The pilot's family –?"

"Yes, of course."

"The refugees?"

"Of course again."

Hair nodded briskly; Hair seemed satisfied. He was capable of amoral action but prided himself on his private conscience. He tapped the file again sharply. "Then what of this?"

"I was going to tell you, or rather what the backroom boys tell me. Whatever the Russians put down on that village it wasn't napalm and it wasn't phosphorus. It was a good deal more deadly than either of those but it wasn't this new thing the Brits have."

"ANNE, you mean. So what *have* the Russians got?"

Wig drew a deliberate breath; he liked to take his time,

hated hustlers. "According to the boffins behind me they've got something more advanced than we have but it's not in the same class as ANNE."

"Evidence?" Hair snapped it.

"Those tanks in that photograph. It wasn't a mistake that they were there. The Russians put them in deliberately, withdrawing the crews before they bombed. Now they're burnt-out shells and they're recovering them for examination."

"And what does that prove?"

"A negative. If what the Russians dropped had been ANNE those tanks would not have been burnt-out hulks. They'd have been shapeless masses of molten metal, probably still too hot to handle."

"That's what your scientists say?"

"In more detail."

"And not a trace of radiation?"

"None."

Hair put on impressive spectacles. He was vain and never wore them in public, reading his alarming speeches from a prompter with letters a quarter-inch high.

"But aren't our own men somewhere near it themselves? We pay scientists almost as much as doctors."

"I cannot speak for the scientists and no doubt you have other reports to guide you but as a simple man understands it simply this ANNE is a bit of a sport."

"A sport?"

"In the anthropomorphic sense – a fluke. The physicists and the mathematicians, the engineers and the men on the fringes of science – they think they are pretty close to it, ready to shout Eureka and go home, and then something doesn't happen to rule and they're back where they started and looking foolish. For the time, that is, and time is important."

Hair put down his spectacles carefully. He wasn't smiling now but looking strong. It was something he practised every morning as he shaved.

"In that case we've got to get hold of it quickly."

"From the British?"

"Who else?"

The man in the grey wig sighed silently. He was going to be asked to do something foolish and instinct and a long experience both recoiled from any sort of foolishness. The last time they had tried an adventure it had ended in humiliation. Aircraft hadn't reached their targets or where they did had somehow contrived to collide on the ground. Transport hadn't turned up nor the promised auxiliaries. The affair had been a risible shambles and America had been mocked around the world. Worst of all they had left their dead behind them.

Wig would rather resign than try that again. He said at his most urbane: "If you say so. Naturally you'll try diplomacy first. The British are our formal allies."

Hair said something about the British which he wouldn't have cared to utter in public. He recovered and said: "They'll ask the earth."

"For what they've got that's not a lot."

"You think so, do you?" It was close to a snarl. The famous practised smile replaced it. "But of course you're right – we'll try bargaining first. But I want an alternative plan in detail, something ready to go if I press the button."

Wig took his leave.

When he had gone Hair poured a long Bourbon. It was something again he eschewed in public but he felt that he had earned it handsomely. He was the most powerful man in the world – the Press said so – but he had more worries than old Job had had sores. As long as he kept control of the Senate he could usually outface the House and had a very fair chance of re-election. His position constitutionally was as powerful as any man's on earth but he couldn't ignore the organised lobbies, the Jewish, the Irish, the blacks, the farmers – the whole damned pack. He could bring enormous pressure on Russia by simply declining to sell her corn again but if he did so he'd lose the prairie States. Or he could settle the turbulent Middle East by pulling the rug from under Israel. In which case the Jewish lobby would raise hell.

There were times when he wished he'd been born in a simpler land.

★

Colonel Charles Russell, lately of the Security Executive, woke early that morning and drank his tea. It was going to be a troublesome day.

Because "lately" expressed the position ambiguously. He had been head of the old Security Executive but had been quietly dropped when the Left had put pressure on, increasing, organised, deadly pressure, the sort of campaign which it ran efficiently – the public protests, the private smears. There'd been an interim of assorted stopgaps, men of various backgrounds and varying competence, but now Russell, like the Stuart kings, was back to the general relief of all sane men.

Not that the Restoration had been absolute. Like the Stuart kings his power had diminished but for that he was duly and properly thankful. Before he had stood alone and vulnerable, as indeed in the end he had proved to be, but now he was protected and buttressed, a member of a powerful committee.

He laughed as he drank his second cup of tea. The previous Prime Minister had detested that word, insisting that the new Executive be simply the Board of a well-run company. She herself would accept the chairmanship, which in practice was only a change on paper, since in a crisis Charles Russell must talk to her anyway, but she wouldn't attend the regular meetings which Russell could run as the Deputy Chairman. Cosy? he had suggested. Yes, very. So three days a week and you can keep up your golf. Much better than another stopgap in a set-up which leant so heavily on flair.

Charles Russell had accepted gladly. Duty and personal inclination for once in his life showed a similar signpost.

But as he shaved he was something less than happy for the meeting of the Board this morning was going to be a difficult hour. It was to be preceded by a full Cabinet confab and Russell had been told its main subject. This was ANNE and Russell frowned uneasily. Advanced Non-Nuclear Explosive – Jesus! Another step into total barbarism. Charles Russell had no knowledge of science but he knew in simple terms what ANNE did. Its blast was inconsiderable and, importantly, it produced no fall-out; it produced instead twenty seconds of heat and this heat was near that of a nuclear big bang. Nothing could hope to survive in it, man or machine, and for the moment Russell's country held it alone.

For the moment – that was where he came in. Charles Russell was not a physicist but he knew just enough of the physicists' world to know there was no such thing as a secret. Or rather not a secret of principle. Of know-how and technology, certainly, and these were jealously guarded everywhere, but top-class scientists moved in line abreast. Whatever their nationality, whatever the efforts at isolation, they seemed to keep in step like soldiers. Russia would have achieved the bomb without assistance from a series of traitors. Nevertheless it would have taken her longer.

That was the point, Russell thought – the time factor; that was where he could help – to extend it. Any one of the developed countries might stumble on ANNE that afternoon, Russia or the United States, France or, God forfend it, Israel. There was nothing he could do about that and nothing he would be asked to do, but whilst his country held this vulnerable secret it held something of advantage which it could trade. It would no more fire an ANNE at an enemy than it would independently fire its alleged deterrent but so long as it held a headstart in time it could exact an enormous price from an ally.

And of course a country which wasn't an ally would want it too and use other means. Spies, it went without saying, and traitors. They were back in the late 'forties when rivals had been trying to cut the time. It was that sort of situation again and Russell was going to be asked to police it.

He never ate an English breakfast unless he were playing golf and needed it but he drank his coffee and ate his croissants, aware he was onto a beating to nothing. Even if he prevented all leaks, and that on past form would be superhuman, some man in a laboratory would be stumbling on the dreadful thing sometime.

Nevertheless he would do his best which wasn't negligible; he had in fact started to do it already. A matter of routine, perhaps, a classic ploy from the orthodox book. But often it was quite effective. Put at its simplest you misled your enemy as Miles Harrison was doing at Yeldham.

Enemy, Russell thought – no, enemies. He knew of only one at the moment – the Americans would try diplomacy first – but if that failed they'd go for something else and when they did it would not be by spying. The Russians always went for that first and very good indeed they were at it, but Americans often tried to cut corners and when they did the game went wide open.

2

In the hierarchy of the Yeldham establishment Miles Harrison ranked just below the top. He was thought of as sound and entirely reliable, the master of every tool of his trade, a natural midwife to the labours of genius. This he was content to be since he knew that where the fire fell from heaven the ordinary first class brain was out of its league. Judith Maxe, his Chief, occasionally received this fire – not often, because the gods gave sparingly – but when she did she could leave him standing. Over ANNE, for instance, which was why she was there. He was a better mathematician than she and had sniffed round ANNE's untidy skirts with disbelief and indeed distaste. Untidy was the word: ANNE offended him. Unfortunately the slut existed, or rather she existed sometimes. And "sometimes" wasn't a word of science. You set up a series of complex reactions, using an amount of power which would have lighted and heated a major city, and sometimes the end product was ANNE. Equally it might be nothing and twice it had been near-disaster.

He was too senior to be watching dials but a fresh charge had just gone in and he was. His juniors were controlling it since by now the process was almost a drill. When it succeeded you had your ANNE, deadly and entirely un-nuclear. Or maybe you had nothing whatever, just an ounce or two of some useless dust. Or maybe you burnt Yeldham to ashes.

In this clinical air-conditioned control room smoking would be out of the question but Harrison told the next senior man he wanted a cigarette. He went to the canteen and ordered coffee; he limited his cigarettes to the number which he really enjoyed.

He relaxed for he had no reason not to: the morning's

operation was going well. He had the income of his rank which was generous and he lived in a house in a nearby development with a wife whose habits suited him perfectly. They had never shared a bedroom, far less a bed, but they covered for each other beautifully. Miles Harrison didn't care for women, they always tried to cut you down to size. He had seen it put as he couldn't better it. Women constantly complained about living in a world made for men but the truth of that was very limited. In the details which enormously multiplied women were omnipotent. No man could withstand the steady friction, the inexhaustible wearing of feminine prejudice. Forever rolled in the resistless stream of women's ambitions men became round and smooth and admirable, like pebbles.

But Miles Harrison's wife did no such thing; she wasn't interested in men nor in altering them. She was a very fair cook and a Doctor of Philosophy and when he went home after work in the evening he could be confident of intelligent chatter. He got up early and she rose late.

They got on together extremely well.

He'd been lucky, he reflected – very. Any man who worked in a Top Secret establishment was subject to Positive Vetting and he knew that he had been positively vetted. Of course he had – he was classically vulnerable – but the vetting had been shrewd as well as tough. He had been quietly told that his tastes were known but they seemed to be controlled and disciplined and none of his friends was suspect himself. He was to watch it, though; he was a tempting target.

When inevitably the approach had come he had known what to do and had done it promptly. He had done it with a real regret for he knew what would happen: they would move him to somewhere less secret and sensitive, by definition somewhere less interesting. Life at Yeldham had suited him perfectly. ANNE exasperated him but it also fascinated. Nevertheless he hadn't hesitated. He was a homosexual but he wasn't a pouffe; he wasn't prepared to live under blackmail.

He had reported to security at once; and waited.

He had waited a surprisingly short time. Next evening a

modest car had arrived and an urbane young man had got
out with a briefcase. "I understand your wife is away."
Evidently he had done his homework.

"My wife is in London."

The urbane young man said politely: "Then may I come
in?"

"Of course. I was expecting you."

They went into the living room and Miles Harrison asked:
"A drink?"

"A little whisky and water, please." He was abundantly
making it clear he was there as a friend. They sat down with
their drinks and the young man asked: "This man who
approached you – you know his name?"

"He gave me one for what that's worth."

"Almost certainly nothing. Can you describe him?"

Miles Harrison noticed detail professionally and the young
man nodded and smiled approval. From his briefcase he
took a photograph.

"That one?"

"I would bet on it."

"Good. His name is Azimev. He works in the Russian
Trade Mission, keeping his head down quietly till something
turns up that's worth a risk."

"Such as myself?"

"I'm afraid that's so."

Miles Harrison thought, then decided to risk it; he wanted
this over and settled for good. "I realise you'll have to move
me elsewhere."

"Not necessarily," the young man said. "In the end it
rather depends on you."

"I'm afraid I don't follow."

The other seemed to be changing the subject. "Have you
any particular feeling for Russians?"

"I respect their scientists and I admire their achievements.
Otherwise I'm entirely indifferent. Politics are not my
hobby. If they were I'd have long ago taken my life."

"Not an uncommon feeling in clever men." The young
man went to his briefcase again, extracting a single sheet of
foolscap. It was covered with mathematical symbols laid out
in a series of complex equations. "I needn't say that I don't

understand this." He passed the sheet over. "The practical point is simply: Do you?"

Miles Harrison took his time with the paper; finally he said deliberately: "I have seen something very like this before."

"You understand it?"

"Understand is an elastic word. As mathematics it is within my competence and in that sense you could say that I understood. What I don't comprehend is why it works, why it produces ANNE. Or sometimes. That is why I like working at Yeldham. It's all infuriatingly unscientific. It's a frontier and a dangerous challenge."

"Then there's no need for us to shift you. There's a basis for a bargain here."

"A bargain?"

"A sort of *quid pro quo*. I'm not senior enough to be able to talk but is your wife staying in London long?"

"She usually stays a week at least."

"Then I'll send a car to fetch you tomorrow. Till tomorrow evening."

A car had arrived as promised and driven Harrison to West Ealing smoothly. It was an area which he had known as a boy and he knew that it had changed remarkably. Once it had been a middle-class suburb – retired officials from a still flourishing Empire, small *rentiers* and successful shop-keepers. Now it was almost a foreign country – Italian waiters in steady jobs, Hong Kong Chinese who kept themselves to themselves and the occasional superior African. But it hadn't yet become a slum. The superior sort of Africans had chased away the despised West Indians.

They stopped at what had once been a villa, now divided, Harrison guessed, into flats. There was a small crescent-shaped drive through untidy laurels, and the driver, who hadn't uttered while driving, got down and let Harrison out politely. He rang the bell and a voice from the speaker said: "Please wait." The door opened on the young man of the previous night. "Kind of you to come," he said. "Come in." He looked at the driver who nodded briefly.

"I'll be back in half an hour as arranged."

The young man led the way upstairs over carpeting which

had worn to the boards. The dados were painted a fading chocolate, the whole aura one of a pinched decay. He knocked on a door and then pushed it open. "Mr Harrison, sir." he said.

He withdrew.

A tall man rose from a tatty armchair, pulling another up for Harrison. "I'm Charles Russell," he said, "of the Security Executive. I used to be the working boss but now I'm called the Deputy Chairman. I'm sorry to have dragged you out here but there are times when we prefer it for interviews. Still, I'm sorry." He waved a hand round the room in explanation. It held the two chairs and a broken-legged sofa. The walls were bare of pictures and peeling. It was bleak.

"I think I understand."

"Thank you."

For a moment the two men sat silent, weighing each other. Charles Russell was seldom photographed and the self-introduction had been more than a courtesy. But Miles Harrison had heard of him and now he looked him over thoughtfully. He liked what he saw and was willing to trust it. This man might hold the rank of Colonel but he was a long way from a military stereotype; his manner was neither old boy nor hearty and he wasn't wearing his regiment's tie. He was in his sixties, perhaps, but he didn't look it and he hadn't a superfluous ounce on his body.

Russell for his part was approving of Harrison. In turn he was not the cut-out scientist. He didn't wear glasses or suspect grey flannels but a well-made suit and well-kept shoes. Excellent turn-out, Charles Russell thought.

"So they've come to you at last," he said. "If I may say so without it sounding impertinent it was more or less bound to happen sometime."

"I suppose it was."

"You suppose correctly." Charles Russell shrugged. The reason wasn't worth discussion. He had the tolerance of his class for other men's tastes. He had never been attracted himself and there it lay. "The question now is what to do."

"I imagine that rests with you."

"Not entirely. The orthodox course would be to move you from Yeldham. Which I gather you would not like."

"Not at all."

"Then would you co-operate?"

"Yes. But how?"

"By feeding the Russians what isn't true. The current cant-word is misinformation."

"Wouldn't that be dangerous?"

"Possibly."

"You must let me think it over, then."

Charles Russell watched him do so confidently for he would have agreed with Miles Harrison's private self-judgement. This man was a homo but he wasn't a pouffe. Too many people assumed that all homos were. Russell had known two in the war and both had been extravagantly brave.

Presently Harrison said: "Tell me how."

"You'll have to listen to a layman talking cock."

Miles Harrison laughed. "No doubt you've been briefed."

"I've been briefed, all right, but I'm only a parrot." Russell felt in a pocket and pulled out a paper; his voice changed into a sort of recital. "There are elements which do not exist in nature though on the molecular scale which is used as a measure there is room for them to exist?"

"That is so."

"But modern nuclear physicists have been able to construct at least two?"

"Correct again," Miles Harrison said.

"One is called Rhysium?"

Harrison hesitated. Rhysium was top Top Secret; Rhysium was the core of Yeldham. He decided to prevaricate. "Rhysium was constructed," (privately he rather fancied the word) "by the eminent Professor Ivor Rhys." He added unnecessarily: "Welsh, of course."

Russell's smile was polite but he went on remorselessly. "And Rhysium is essential to ANNE." This time it wasn't put as a question.

Harrison thought this over carefully; he was astonished that Russell should know but he did. He had said he'd been briefed and he clearly had. Harrison wondered by whom but he needn't know. He said non-committally:

"Since you say so."

Charles Russell let this pass without comment; he consulted his paper again and asked: "What would happen if you used something else? Another of these fancy new elements?"

This one Miles could answer easily. "I haven't an idea on earth."

"Would it produce an ANNE?"

"Improbable. But I'm a scientist and I can't say it wouldn't."

"But possibly something akin?"

"A guess."

Russell put his paper away. "The point of these blunderings is basically simple. These new elements are esoteric knowledge. If you told a foreign scientist that, say, One-Six-Seven was used to make ANNE he wouldn't laugh in your face nor suspect a decoy?"

"In his place I wouldn't."

"I'm delighted to hear it. For a decoy is what we plan – to buy time. We want the Russians to put their pack on a false scent. You hint that it mightn't be wholly false but that's a risk we're prepared to accept." Russell looked at Harrison levelly. "Will you do it?" he asked.

"While I stay on at Yeldham? It's really another sort of blackmail."

Charles Russell held a hand up. "No, not directly. It's been decided that you stay there anyway but of course we should have to watch you day and night. At Yeldham or anywhere else you chose to go."

"It's still a kind of blackmail."

"A mild one." A pause. "Will you do as I ask?"

"I will for the hell of it."

"The best possible reason. I distrust men who work for political motives." Russell became immediately practical. "When did Azimev say he was coming back?"

"He didn't."

"That's perfectly normal. But when he does he'll give you a drop. That's tired old jargon for a place to leave messages. I doubt if you'll see him again after that."

"It's as simple as that?"

"If the business goes well."

"Are you hinting it may not?"

"Not exactly. But I wouldn't employ a double agent, and that is what in effect you now are, without telling him it's a dangerous trade."

This scene had come back to Miles Harrison vividly as he drank his morning coffee and smoked his cigarette. He would have liked another but he counted his pack. He'd had five that morning and that was his ration.

He was walking back along the glassed-in corridor when a man appeared at the other end. He was overweight and running clumsily and when he saw Miles he shouted: "Come."

Miles Harrison began to run too. He didn't ask questions for he had guessed what was happening.

In the control room the tension was sharp, almost tangible. Men and women stood in groups, not talking, waiting for a final decision. When the siren went they would know what to do. They would go to their flashproof underground bunker – they sincerely hoped it would prove to be flashproof – and there they would wait till the All Clear sounded or till something quite unthinkable happened. They practised it every week like a boat drill at sea.

Their heads turned like disciplined puppets as Miles came in. He went to the chair which he'd left for his morning break and sat down. The two master dials were in a console before him and the pointers of both had moved critically upwards. The left measured the torrent of power pouring in and Harrison wasn't fearful of this. Beyond a certain point it would cut itself out. But the second dial was not reassuring. The charge was getting alarmingly hot, the reactor was burning too fast by far.

"Reactor", he thought on a sudden irrelevance, was a word they tried to avoid on principle. It was used in nuclear physics freely and one thing which ANNE was not was nuclear. It was fickle and extremely unstable and when you got it right it was deadly but the point, the political point when you faced it, was that there wasn't the faintest trace of fall-out. Nothing could live where ANNE fell and that was that. But you wouldn't poison a million people.

Harrison looked at the dial on the right again. It had risen but had a point to go before it reached the red and decided for him. He looked at a smaller vernier. It had stopped. Call Judith Maxe, the Chief, and pass the buck? But she mightn't be easy to find at this moment. Up in the big house behind him Dick Maxe had come down from his Norfolk acres and Judith would be giving a party. She would probably simply tell him to play it safe.

Which it went against the grain to do. Every time you accepted a charge from the physicists, every time you set up the elaborate process, every time you burnt up enough power to light Birmingham . . .

Every time you did these things it cost the country a great deal of money. Miles Harrison was a Scot and provident.

But his hand was on the alarm when he looked again. The main dial hadn't moved but the vernier had. Very slowly it was coming down.

He waited, watching the big one. It slipped a point.

Miles Harrison let his breath out softly; he said to the stout man, the next in command: "That was a pretty close shave."

"Too close."

3

Arthur Milden looked round the Cabinet room, more than a little surprised at being there. The recent palace revolution had made a pretty clean sweep of the likes of Milden: the Hard Right was out and the Soft Right back again, the pragmatists, the Knights of the Shires, the men who had married in old Tory families. The previous Prime Minister had fought like a tiger but the huge pressure of this ancient tide had submerged her in the 'end and for good. Being the sort of people they were, it hadn't been done with open malice. The Prime Minister had been permitted to depart. It had all been on the face of it generous but also it had been beautifully calculated by men who had been through revolts before.

Arthur Milden had been the former Prime Minister's man, sharing her simple, abrasive philosophy. The country was as soft as putty, the Keynesian ethic rotting its viscera, and one couldn't go on fluffing for ever. The answer was back to the marketplace quickly, the simple virtues of the sensible housewife . . . Deficit financing, consensus politics? Heresies. Cancers in the body politic. And they wouldn't just go away, you must use the knife. Look at those outrageous Trades Unions, look at the Old School Ties on the other side. Less than there had been, perhaps, but still powerful. Jesus what a mess to have to clear up! And what did you get for your pains when you tried to? You got talk of something called confrontation, about the silliest word in the political lexicon.

With most of this Arthur Milden had agreed, yet here he was in the Cabinet room, kept in office by men who thought wholly otherwise. Consensus men. He despised them heartily.

His presence needed some explanation and Milden had

reached one he thought was reasonable. It was based on a misapprehension and made him laugh, for the misapprehension wasn't his own but that of his woolly-minded colleagues. None had a scientific training and "scientist" simply meant boffin, a man who had. There had been Scientific Advisers to governments before and their record had been entirely disastrous. One had killed a fighter-bomber which would have given Great Britain a lead of a decade, and in aviation ten years was a very long time. Another had simply stated *ex cathedra* that the human body could not withstand Mach-plus flight. So here Milden was in a minor Ministry, a tame-cat pundit to answer the questions. He knew the subject of this morning's meeting. It was ANNE and he'd been called in to explain.

And he couldn't explain, it wasn't his discipline. Yeldham was technically part of his Ministry but all he knew of research at Yeldham was his great relief that he wasn't working there.

ANNE was extremely unstable and dangerous.

The Very Senior Legal Figure was a little late, something which he contrived on principle, but the Prime Minister was waiting patiently. Milden looked at him and didn't admire him but he conceded him the points he deserved. He was the ringer of a late Field Marshal, the same foxy face and a nose for the odds. He wouldn't take any action whatever if the chances weren't three to one in his favour. But there the resemblance ended dead. He didn't bark like a dog nor boast in public. Foxy was smart but a civilised operator. He had charm when he needed it and otherwise a vicious bite.

The VSLF arrived at last, nodding a little patronisingly at the Prime Minister to whom he owed his post. He didn't privately see it that way since to have dropped him would have been inconceivable. He was the sheet-anchor of the Old Tory ship, as much a part of its ethos as cricket. The Prime Minister watched him take his seat, continuing to chat smoothly of nothing. He was waiting for the old man to nod off. Awake he was tiresomely prone to homily.

So Foxy talked on but watched the VSLF. The noble old head had begun to droop; a tiny stream of saliva ran out of

27

the mouth. When it fell on the blotter Foxy spoke.

"Business, ladies and gentlemen. ANNE." Foxy looked straight at Milden, then seemed suddenly to change his mind. "I had considered asking Mr Milden to open, to give us an outline of what happens at Yeldham, but on reflection I think that might be a waste of time."

Milden in turn looked hard at Foxy. The words had been deliberately ambiguous – whose time would be wasted and wasted by whom? – but Milden had caught the clear echo of malice. He had heard it before from these men who disliked him but not so far from this smooth Prime Minister.

Who was going on quietly as though he'd said nothing. "So let's move to the practical aspect – the bargaining. We have ANNE and the Americans have not. They have asked for it and we've asked a price. Over to you, Foreign Secretary, please."

Lord George nodded briefly and started to speak. His ancestors had settled in England, followers of Dutch William the Third, marrying heiresses, thriving mightily, climbing up the peerage steadily. Three centuries of English life had sharpened his wits and refined his manners but Dutch genes were strong and extremely persistent and in a crisis he had an immovable stubbornness. He ran the Foreign Office perfectly, standing no nonsense from hoity-toity officials, dealing firmly with the still rampant pro-Arabism, but he would listen to advice when it was good. With foreign envoys he was wholly admirable; he didn't attempt to bully them but nor would he cringe to some African upstart. He was a man of wealth and a ruthless negotiator.

Milden looked at him with a real respect. He wasn't Milden's sort of man but he had something which he himself had not. He had roots. Arthur Milden had cut his own and felt the loss.

The Foreign Secretary was talking crisply. "You mentioned a price and indeed we have asked one. Put in its simplest form it is this: we have asked for an end to all aid to the IRA. Not so much weapons which are still getting through but to the formidable sums of money which buy them, the more or less voluntary contributions which private Americans make from their private purses. They may not go at once or directly to people who are known to be terrorists but the cover is alarmingly good and they reach them in the end. To buy weapons."

"And what did the Americans say?"

"They were regretful, they were sympathetic, but they said that they couldn't do that. Constitutionally."

Foxy turned to the Law Officer present. He wasn't a full Cabinet member but like Milden was called when a matter concerned him. He was a nervous little man and with reason. He was a Queen's Counsel, since he'd been long in Parliament, but aware that his Silk was artificial, and his standing in his own profession fell far short of his official position. His professional peers thought him sound but naif, somewhere around the average standard of a competent provincial solicitor. He collected his thoughts and said at length:

"The American system is not like ours. They have separation of powers – executive, judicial, legislative. We live under a parliamentary dictatorship."

The VSLF caught the phrase and for a moment woke. It was one of his remaining hobby horses. "What was that?"

"An aside. Please forget it."

The old man went back to sleep with a soft sigh.

Lord George had cut in again, curtly, decisively. The legal niceties bored him cruelly. Lawyers were people who did what you told them.

"I don't think it's the legal side which really makes the President hesitate. That has been got round before and I haven't a doubt it could be again. What worries him is the coming election. No president hoping for re-election can afford to throw the Irish vote against him."

Foxy nodded again as he thought this over. Like Lord George he thought very little of lawyers. "Then what are you going to do?"

"I? Nothing. I shall sit on my hands till the Americans come back to me. They want ANNE badly – they'll offer *something*."

"Any idea what it's going to be?"

"I could guess but I'm not going to – not now. But you

can be perfectly sure of one thing, Prime Minister. Whatever it is I shall have my instructions."

. . . There's something very odd going on Milden thought. "Whatever it is I shall have my instructions." Of course he'll have his damned instructions, they'll have been agreed at a Cabinet meeting proper from which I was equally properly absent. But the way he said it. . .

He doesn't much like them.

The Cabinet ended with minor business but Milden didn't rise with the others. He had been asked to stay and attend the Board, the successor to the old Executive, and he noticed that Lord George had too. This was the meeting which Russell had feared as likely to be both fierce and unfruitful.

The Prime Minister led the way to another room, smaller and a good deal less formal. There were flowers on handsome Georgian tables, a fireplace with a log fire burning, and in the corner what was clearly a bar. The Prime Minister went to it.

"Refreshments, gentlemen. Colonel Russell will help me."

He waved at the other three men who had risen. He disapproved of Christian names except in families and with very close friends and he said as he set up the drinks: "Lord George and Milden – I think you've already met Charles Russell." He introduced the man who had troubled to put on uniform as the Commissioner of Metropolitan Police and an eminent figure drinking pink gin as a retired High Court judge. The Judge was a man of immense erudition and a reputation for leaning Left. Which he did not. There was a fifth member of the Board but he was absent. "I understand he's engaged in ordaining clergy."

As he chatted easily, relaxing tension, an experienced political brain was working. The previous Prime Minister had been a reluctant delegator; she'd had no need to take on the formal chairmanship of this Board which was now the Security Executive since the crises came up to her, like it or not. But the idea of a Board and the men she had put on it had shown political skill at the highest level. It had enabled Charles Russell's unmatched experience to be used as it should be, in active counsel, without binding the man to a nine-to-five desk. And Jack Pallant, the Commissioner who carried the can for the city's race riots, had been a choice of wisdom. Subversion in its widest sense was the Executive's daily meat and drink and subversion in its most scaring form was endemic in several boroughs of London. It was convenient that the Commissioner be privy to the Executive's thinking and in any case he'd been Russell's close friend.

The other two members were there for their names, a sop to the still vocal Left. The Judge was a man of the solid Right but had earned himself almost a cult reputation with the woollier sort of intellectual. He had been trying a black for murdering a policeman and the evidence had been open and shut. Except that Me Lud had scented fish. He hadn't a doubt that the man was guilty and as a citizen he'd had even less doubt that he'd be better out of the way for some time. But if irregular things were done, as he knew they were, you musn't offend a judge's nostrils. That job must be perfectly done or not at all.

He had used his enormous erudition to stand the evidence firmly on its head. His summing up had left the jury no option.

Next day he had become a hero to people he had never heard of. He didn't mind that, he was shortly retiring, and it had brought him into contact with a new world. The pale people – the last Prime Minister's word for them. He had seen through them at once as shams but he was a bachelor and threatened with loneliness. Now he was a respected figure in a world which never ceased to amuse him.

The fifth appointment, absent that morning, had been even more a choice of cosmetics. It was Bill Basingstoke, the with-it bishop, the idol of every rebel without a cause. He had attended twice and been voted down heavily but he hadn't resigned, he had huffed off offended. The post was worth several thousand a year. So his name was still there as a full-fledged director, a false comfort to all progressive thinkers.

So six men now sat in the comfortable room. Four of them were there by right, the Prime Minister, Russell, Jack

Pallant and the judge. The other two were Lord George and Milden who'd been invited because as Ministers they were inescapably concerned with ANNE. The atmosphere by now was easy and those who had wanted second drinks had them. They sat in comfortable chairs, in no particular order, and when he saw they were ready Foxy spoke.

"The agenda, as usual, has not been recorded but I think we all know what we have to discuss. Mr Milden and Lord George are here because there've been developments which concern them directly."

He made a gesture with a very clean hand. Some late Ministers' hands had not always been perfect and Foxy had admitted in private, in fact in the matrimonial bed, that these less than immaculate nails had had their weight. The last Prime Minister had become intolerable, both arrogant and a slave to doctrine, but Foxy had fought in a war with distinction and might have hesitated about what amounted to mutiny against Ministers who'd been parade-ground clean. Now he waved at Lord George.

"All yours."

"I'll do my best."

Lord George discarded three centuries smoothly, reverting to his Dutch fathers shamelessly; he became blunt and direct and at times near-offensive and he made it as clear as a Dutchman could that he considered this lack of finesse a virtue. "America wants our ANNE very badly and I don't doubt the Russians want it too. The Russians don't negotiate, or not until they're forced to a table, but I'm negotiating with the Americans presently. My hand depends on the strength of monopoly, the fact that we alone have ANNE. The Americans wouldn't pay much for a secret shared. Security is therefore paramount and I can say here what I couldn't in Cabinet. I suspect there may have been a leak."

He broke off to refresh himself and the judge behind his pink gin said: "Go on."

"By your leave, then, it goes something like this." Lord George outlined the report of the burnt Afghan village. "The Russians don't have ANNE, or not yet, but the Russians do have something quite nasty. I told you I was scared and I am."

Lord George was an experienced committee man who knew when to pause to let words sink in, and Milden used the moment to think. He was glad that he hadn't been asked to be technical on a subject of which he knew next to nothing but he was Minister of a minor Department and in the title of that Department was "Science". That might or it might not be ominous. One thing was as sure as next day's dawn.He was odd beastie out in this lush Tory meadow.

Foxy was feeding the ball back neatly. Looking at Lord George he asked:

"So you suspect there has been a breach of security?"

"I'm not concerned with security as such, and in this company I may say I'm glad of it. I'm concerned with a desperate hand of poker with people who've made it their national game."

"So if the Russians got ANNE first –?"

"The game would stop."

"They might, you know – quite apart from leaks." It was the judge and he was being judicial. "Perhaps they've been successfully spying but there's another explanation we shouldn't rule out." He put into words what Charles Russell had thought. "All top scientists seem to move together, even when not allowed to communicate. Give them the sort of things they need, laboratories and a great deal of money, and a man who's been working away in Maine will come up with much the same result as his peer who's been running the same scent in Moscow. Not exactly the same perhaps, but near enough. And not exactly at the same moment of time." The judge looked at Milden and neatly included him. "Would you agree with that, Mr Milden?"

"I'm very much afraid I must."

Lord George said sharply: "Time. So I haven't got un-limited time. If some spy doesn't dish my hand some scientist may."

"Just about that," the Prime Minister said. He risked a glance at Charles Russell who looked away. The two of them shared a necessary secret. It wasn't the sort of thing for a Board, far less to spray round the Cabinet room.

"I'm seeing the American ambassador tomorrow." Lord

33

George, it was clear, was not looking forward to it. "I much prefer to deal with professionals and this one's the other sort – every inch so. Enormous gifts to party funds and a wife who's a successful hostess."

"What are you going to ask of him?"

"Nothing, or rather nothing at first. As I told you I'm going to hear what he offers. We've come to the end of that IRA thing. With an election not so far in the distance no President would risk the votes. And as I mentioned before I'll have instructions to guide me."

There it goes for the second time, Milden thought. I wonder why.

"Will you tell him that ANNE's untamed – unstable?" It was the judge and he was again judicial.

"Of course I shan't. It would weaken my hand."

Arthur Milden looked hard at the Foreign Secretary. In the simple world he had turned his back on the omission would be plain dishonest. But then he wasn't the son of a great house; he wasn't even a mainstream Tory.

"Then I think that's all for the moment." The Prime Minister rose. He went to the door to see them out and as Russell went past him his social smile sharpened. "Quite a good meeting, I think. Don't you?"

"It might have been a lot more awkward. But there's something I'd like to mention."

"Here?"

"A matter of routine. Curiosity. You know, I've never been to Yeldham in my life."

"Then certainly you should go. At once." Foxy beckoned to Milden who came over politely. "Colonel Russell would like to visit Yeldham. I'd be grateful if you'd take him. Tomorrow."

"I've engagements all tomorrow, Prime Minister."

"I expect you could contrive to postpone them." He turned to Russell. "The morning suits you?"

"Perfectly, thank you."

"Then that's arranged."

Russell went home in a taxi reflectively. It had been one of the sharpest snubs he had ever heard. They hadn't wished to sweep too clean or not in a single morning's sweeping, so they'd left Arthur Milden as a sop to the hard men. But he was a maverick in this High Tory caucus. They would drop him when they were ready. Flat.

4

Charles Russell had gone to Number Ten fearful that something outside his own orbit might be obliging Foxy to share with others the knowledge that they'd been buying time by a method which might not appeal to self-righteous men. Foxy, after all, wore two hats: he was Chairman of the Executive's Board and on top of that he was also Prime Minister. It wasn't inconceivable that in the world of the latter, which wasn't Russell's, something had happened to force his hand. But no, they'd exchanged a glance and that was all.

Russell had left relieved but curious – curious about Arthur Milden. He had spoken when asked a question directly and at the end had been brutally snubbed by Foxy. Charles Russell had thought that entirely unnecessary. The recent palace revolution had swept the old True Blues back to power, the men of inherited wealth and position, the men with connections in banking and brewing. Arthur Milden was clearly not one of these but they'd decided to keep him, at any rate temporarily, and as long as they chose to they owed him the courtesies. The Prime Minister had lost points with Charles Russell.

He went to his club and lunched alone, then took a taxi to the Security Executive. He no longer needed to go there daily but there was a room for Board members to use when they wished to and in it he said to the man who had met him: "I'd like a print-out of Arthur Milden, please. And another on Judith Maxe who runs Yeldham."

He'd be meeting her with Milden tomorrow and he believed in careful briefing beforehand.

He started on Milden and nodded, satisfied. His background did not belie his manner. His family was solid army, the sort which had had to fight the real battles when flash

36

cavalry in untried armour, flying pennants to show they were different people, had charged onto minefields and Eighty-Eights.

He broke off with a smile for "solid army" was suspect. Pronounce such a phrase and you'd be branded a snob. It was deplorable how words changed their meaning. In his youth the word snob had meant only one thing, a man who sought the friendship or company of persons who were above him in station, but nowadays if you even admitted that classes, obstinately, still existed the chic Left would raise disdainful eyebrows.

And there was another distinction of fact which you dare not make. *Pace* the social engineers men were not in fact born equal. They varied in talent as they varied in weight. But record such a thing in speech or writing and the fashionable word was élitist. And of course to speak of race was unthinkable. Even to suggest indirectly that the average West Indian was not as bright as the average Frenchman and a whole establishment, kept at public expense, would be dropping its load on your head next morning. You could be fined or even sent to prison. Racism was the worst word of all, especially since it meant nothing whatever.

Charles Russell returned to the print-out with a shrug. He had an almost feminine mistrust of abstractions and he went back to Arthur Milden with relief.

So he'd been earmarked for the army from birth and at first he hadn't kicked against the pricks. Anything had been better than his graceless little southern school, grimly wedded to muscular faith and sound doctrine, hopelessly ensnared by athletics, the runnings, hoppings, skippings and jumpings before the games which Arthur liked and played reasonably. It had been before the days of direct army sponsorship but a clever boy had wanted a university first and his school had a closed exhibition to Cambridge. Arthur had worked hard and won it. He could go to whichever college would have him provided he made the army his career.

But in the event he had escaped the army ("escaped" was the print-out's word, not Russell's) for away from the country prison he called his school Arthur Milden had come alive and blossomed. The Principal of St. Aidan's college had been a type which by then was becoming rare and later became as dead as the dodo, an academic of the highest class, cranky and quirky and a fine judge of wine. He hated to see a talent wasted and privately was a wealthy man. One day he had sent for Arthur Milden.

. . . He was going to get a first class degree. Had he really set his heart on the army? The Principal had offered a glass of marsala. He had taken a fancy to Arthur Milden. He had expected a plodder. Instead of which he had caught a flyer, a man who might go anywhere later and in a field in which his College was not well known. The Principal was a Good College Man and he hated to see a fine brain underemployed.

He had given Milden a second marsala, then told him that he needn't worry. He had been at St. Aidan's two years, had he not? What he'd drawn from his school in those years was known and would be refunded the next morning promptly. As for the remaining year the Principal would assume the charges. Milden's mother gave him a little too but not enough to take full advantage of the life which St. Aidan's unsensationally offered? That also would be looked after. Good Morning.

Subsequently this had attracted attention as the great Cambridge spy scandals broke in the headlines and the print-out had something to say on this. Charles Russell had skimmed it without much interest. He had met the Principal of St. Aidan's twice and had admired him for the ripe eccentric he was. It had been right to check, though the big birds had flown, but one thing that quirky old man had not been and that was a recruiter of spies.

Nor yet of further pure academics. Arthur Milden had been offered a lectureship with the near-certainty of a fellowship afterwards but the Principal had dissuaded him strongly. St. Aidan's had many distinguished men in the world which he himself adorned but it hadn't spawned a Cabinet Minister for longer than the old man thought seemly. He had used his private connections effectively and Milden had joined an expanding firm whose interests were all things both new and electrical. By thirty-five he had reached its Board, comfortably to do and established, and the Principal, though by now retired, had again pulled the strings of a wealthy man's world. A by-election had offered a seat and Arthur Milden had been selected and won it.

And in Parliament he had again risen steadily, speaking on subjects he understood, the great contracts abroad and how to win them. The former Prime Minister had noticed him and had pushed him up the ladder quietly. Charles Russell was not at all surprised. He mistrusted all popular jargon words but if he had to find one for Milden he easily could. Arthur Milden was the essential meritocrat, the breed which the old gang had just swept away. But they'd left him or at least left him temporarily. That was distinctly odd but explicable.

Charles Russell put the print-out down and smiled. He'd be meeting this man tomorrow morning and was greatly looking forward to doing so. Whatever you said of a man like Milden you could not say that he'd under-achieved.

Russell's hand was on the second print-out when on an instinct he withdrew it suddenly. He'd be meeting Judith Maxe at Yeldham but he knew something of her background already and he decided that he'd meet her first. With men you did your homework carefully, then married that to the experience of meeting them. With women it was often better to meet them first and read them up later. He gave the print-outs back and left the Executive. Tomorrow was going to be more than interesting.

Charles Russell had left the meeting relieved but Arthur Milden in a furious temper. He knew well what the old gang thought of him, but none of this excused a plain rudeness, especially from men who valued good manners. Or was that only amongst themselves? In his taxi home Arthur Milden shrugged. Very well, he'd be difficult; he'd ride it out; he'd ride it till they forced him out. He could probably go back to his firm, though hardly on the Board immediately, or his professional reputation was high, he could set himself up as a private consultant. But he couldn't go back to his roots – he had cut them. His roots were a widowed mother whom he maintained, a dim little school where he hadn't been happy and a marriage which had failed disastrously.

Damn the old gang to hell and he'd help to heat it. He was a middle class man and was going to behave like one.

He opened the door of his flat but checked his stride. A young woman was seated but didn't rise. She stubbed out her cigarette but too late. He had already caught the reek of cannabis.

"Hullo, Peggy."

"Hullo, father."

She hadn't called him Daddy for several years. She still had a key and occasionally called on him but they had drifted apart into different worlds. He gave her an allowance still, since it saved her from the worst of her follies, but when she visited him it was mostly for money and once it had been for a purpose he hated. He hoped that it wasn't that again.

She had taken a whisky and he poured one himself. "How's Parliament?" she asked. She made it sound like a Mafia meeting for she didn't approve of parliamentary democracy.

"Parliament's much the same," he said.

"It was a serious question." He could see that he'd offended her; he was always getting her back up unnecessarily.

"If you mean the House my answer was accurate. It's still full of people I know you detest. If you mean the Cabinet that has changed greatly. It's now full of people whom *I* detest."

"Then why do you stay?"

From this girl of nineteen whose milieu he thought degenerate the question was too near the quick. He gave her a glance of sudden anger but she didn't drop her eyes. "You could call it bloodymindedness."

"Sometimes, father, I'm close to liking you."

They chatted for some minutes of trifles and this time she didn't ask for money. Her present boy friend was wholly exceptional; her present boy friend had a regular job. Secretly she rather despised him. He wasn't even like father, a pitiless Right, a slave to the new golden calf as revealed; he was thoroughly bourgeois and coolly fair-minded . . .

That concentration camp they called South Africa? But, after all, the whites had built it up.

When she rose he held the door politely. "Nice to see you," she said indifferently.

"Come again."

He went back to his drink with a troubled frown, humbly conscious of a private failure. A man should do more for his only daughter than make her a small allowance on time and extract her from her numerous scrapes. The world she moved in he thought was futile – fringe publishing and strange societies, various but with one thing in common. They hated the established order. They paid her much less than she could have earned in a business for when she chose she was an efficient secretary. But when he had tried to wean her away all he'd done had been to increase her contempt for him.

He wasn't very clever with women.

Of course her mother's genes were strong but that was no excuse whatever. He had just made his first really big commission and Maureen had been very attractive. She had told him that she was Anglo-Irish and Milden had known what that meant perfectly: it meant centuries of life in Ireland, marrying into similar families and never a drop of Irish blood. But Maureen hadn't been Anglo-Irish, she'd been a cut-out of the typed stage Irishwomen, fickle and fey and unable to cope. She never got it right alone and when you quietly fixed it for her you had to pretend that you hadn't done so.

She was dead of the bottle. Another failure.

Now her daughter was slipping and he simply wasn't equipped to help her. He was ashamed of his next thought but he let it run. He had been in Russia a year for his firm and though he hadn't liked it he'd been impressed. So he wasn't a very senior Minister but he was a member of what you might call the praesidium and in Russia he could have dealt with Peggy. He could have put her under care and discipline, re-education in sensible values, and his money could have bought the best. He wasn't wealthy but he had made enough.

Enough to have failed with his women utterly.

He put these thoughts aside as unfruitful, thinking of the next day instead. It would be pleasant to talk to Colonel Charles Russell whom he'd liked at sight and was prepared to like more; and it would be pleasant to meet Judith Maxe again.

Or would it? he wondered; he wasn't sure. Their affair had been sudden and fierce and total but they had parted on a flaming quarrel.

No, he wasn't very clever with women and there were certainly things they did better in Russia.

5

Next morning Milden called for Russell and drove him down to the Yeldham establishment. Russell noticed that the car was his own, not a fading hack from some Ministry's pool. Cars could tell you much about men and this one said money but not gross wealth; and the way men drove them told even more. Arthur Milden lost little time but he read the road; he made his decisions quickly and seldom changed them.

Through London, to Russell's approval, he didn't talk, but once on the motorway, fast but watchful, he began to relax in the explanation he felt he owed. "I hope you won't feel that you've wasted your morning. There's precious little to see at Yeldham. It isn't a manufacturing plant. What we do is to take something in and process it."

"Rhysium," Charles Russell said.

For a second the car's speed slackened perceptibly, then picked up again as Milden recovered. He'd been astonished and for a moment shocked for that word was very seldom spoken. Finally he said: "So you know that, do you?" His voice and his manner were equally neutral.

"I know because I know where it comes from. Getting it from there to Yeldham involves a bit more than a guarded convoy – the sort of thing I usually hear about."

Arthur Milden had laughed at that. "Then you may be disappointed this morning. If you know where Rhysium is put together you'll know just about as much as I do. I'm not a physicist, though Judith Maxe is. You'll be meeting her, of course. She's a flyer."

"It sounds very mysterious."

"That's a very good word. I think of it as a sort of alchemy. Sometimes it works and as often it doesn't. And when it doesn't it's pretty dangerous. Have you heard of the vapour bomb?"

"Only the words."

"It doesn't matter, it came to little, but the basic idea was startlingly simple. You created a cloud of tiny particles of something which was highly inflammable, then you fired the cloud and burnt anything under it. ANNE does just that but a thousand times better."

"A formidable weapon."

"Extremely. And politically a potential asset."

"Lord George struck me as being a pretty slick operator."

"He's that, all right, and something to spare. I rather admire him. In fact he's the only one I do."

"You're being very frank."

"Why not? You'll have noticed from yesterday's little incident that I'm not exactly a favourite son."

"May I be equally frank?"

"By all means."

"Then why don't you go before they push you?"

"Good question, that – my daughter once asked it. I was happy enough with the last Prime Minister. She made several mistakes but things got done. I was with people of my own kind whom I trusted. You could say that I felt I was pulling my weight and I approved of where the boat was going after years of half-baked tacking about. Now the old lot's back and they make me despair. So why don't I leave them? It's hard to say. There's nothing noble in it, though – be sure of that. There's nothing of feeling I ought to serve on and nothing of ambition whatever. But rats leave sinking ships and I'm not a rat. They sometimes treat me as though I were but I'm not. Call it simple, old fashioned, blind bloodymindedness."

"Which is often as good a motive as any."

They fell into a momentary silence. Charles Russell was remembering Harrison who'd agreed to what he'd been told might be dangerous, giving as his motive the hell of it; and now Milden was talking of bloodymindedness. Charles Russell had begun to like him: he wouldn't accept second best in any form. Such men made very uneasy bedfellows, you didn't choose them as regular company, but "bloodymindedness" struck a private chord. Charles Russell had spent the best years of his life in propping up a creaking establishment but he wasn't at heart an establishment man. An establishment figure – yes, undeniably – but he had spat in its eye more than once and enjoyed it.

He returned the conversation to Yeldham. "I was interested when you used the word alchemy."

"You thought it ill-chosen?"

"No, not at all. I gather that ANNE doesn't always come out right. When something happens on Monday morning and doesn't happen on Saturday evening – given, that is, a strictly similar process – you're well outside the accepted rules."

"You are indeed and I don't understand it. All I do understand is that the process needs power, enormous amounts of electrical power. You can't take that from the ordinary system, you'd blow everything for miles if you tried, so Yeldham has its own arrangements. My own firm handled that, as it happens, and I was in charge of the operation. That was naturally when I wasn't a Minister. So all I really know about ANNE is that to produce it or, as you say, to fail to, you need more power than you'd use for a railway."

"You apply that power to Rhysium?"

Milden waited some time before he answered; he said at length, and his voice was impersonal: "I suppose you could put it like that if you had to."

. . . He knows more than he says but not the whole story. *Nobody* knows the whole story – not yet. They're not yet in control, they're still experimenting. Sometimes it comes out right and at others . . .

But Milden was explaining on smoothly. "As you know I'm not a physicist but Judith Maxe is just that and more. She'll lay things out much better than I can."

. . . If she chooses to which she probably won't . . .

"I'm looking forward to meeting her," Russell said.

"You haven't before? An extraordinary woman with an extraordinary story. But I expect you know her background."

"Not in detail."

45

"Would you care for a briefing before you meet her?"

"Very much," Russell said. The story from a colleague would be livelier than any dossier.

Milden nodded and collected his thoughts.

"She was born in one of those Baltic states which Mencken called international nuisances. But that was before there were statelings like Malta. Her family was fairly orthodox Jewish and when the Germans took the country over they got away to Sweden in a boat which nearly sank. Judith was only a child at the time but she was one of those mathematical prodigies. That leads naturally to the higher physics and by the time she was in her early twenties Judith had a reputation and a respectable job in a university. But she liked neither Sweden nor university life and in that country a job in the world she wanted is not exactly common or easy to get. So she went to France and later to England where Sir Matthew took her up and pushed her. Now she is one of the top half dozen and officially working for me at Yeldham. As she works in a field which I don't understand, "officially" is just about right. She's very independent, in any case."

"And her husband – is he Jewish too?"

Arthur Milden had laughed again at that. "Nothing could be more the opposite. He's a substantial farmer in darkest Norfolk. He owns his land and there's quite a lot of it. In any other county he'd be a squire. He had the capital to modernise and Dick Maxe is doing nicely, thank you."

"So I shan't be meeting him?"

"As it happens you will. He comes down to Yeldham at least once a fortnight and this is one of the times he'll be there. Judith hardly ever goes to Norfolk but the arrangement seems to work very well. He's an intelligent man with a fair degree. He's twenty years older than she is. You'll be meeting them both in a matter of minutes."

They had moved off the motorway, heading south. The traffic was thinning as the countryside thickened. Arthur Milden asked: "You got that pass?"

"Thank you for sending it." It had in fact arrived the night before.

"I can issue them and naturally did so but they have to be countersigned by Defence."

46

Charles Russell was impressed. This was tight.

So it should be.

They had stopped at park gates with twin lodges beside them. A man came out and looked at their passes. He said into his walkie-talkie: "The Minister and a Colonel Charles Russell." He touched his cap and waved the car on.

Charles Russell was surprised but said nothing for Milden was already explaining. "Yeldham isn't one of the great local houses but for its size the park is pretty big. Too big for our needs or for proper security so we put the fence where a fence made sense. And it's a proper fence with a perimeter road *outside*. Watch-towers every two-fifty yards, each of them in sight of the other."

"And with a proper field of fire?"

"If it came to that but I don't think it will. We learnt a lot from Greenham Common. I doubt if that could happen here. That perimeter road is patrolled intensively and there are other deterrents I don't have to mention."

They had reached the perimeter fence and a blockhouse and two MoD policemen came out and checked them again. The senior smiled at Arthur Milden.

"I'm sorry, sir, but you know the drill."

They were put through a metal-detector briskly and Russell noticed the flash as a camera snapped him. As they moved away again he nodded. "Thorough," he said.

"But not the end of it. There'll be another spot check before we reach the house."

They were now on the inner drive to the manor, banks of rhododendrons on either side. Two men came out of them suddenly in a rush. They were soldiers in battle order, armed. They stopped the car and came closer watchfully. The officer clearly recognised Milden but he looked at Colonel Russell hard. To Milden he said: "Good morning, sir."

"A very good morning."

"I understand your friend has been cleared."

Arthur Milden looked back at the officer's radio. "If you haven't been told that you'd better arrest us."

The officer grinned. "That was part of the drill. Gentlemen you may proceed. My apologies."

As they moved on a third time Milden told Russell: "Officially they're here for training but the training seems to last a long time."

They had arrived at the house and stopped in front of it but Milden made no move to get down. "It's a waste of time to ring the bell. Nobody will move a finger till the last of those three All Clears comes through." He was showing some signs of irritation but Russell was entirely approving.

He used the delay to inspect the manor. It was in the English classical manner but not grand, beautifully proportioned but deliberately modest, the type which James Wyatt had built so well. Where the land sloped away to the right was a lake, an island at its centre invitingly. Milden noticed Charles Russell's inspection.

"Most of that house is now an office but there isn't a lot of paperwork here and there's still room for a flat for Judith Maxe and a room for whoever is duty officer. The rest of the staff lives out and is glad to. Most of what you might call the business end is hidden by those trees." He pointed. "It's modern and unreasonably ugly, made worse by two appalling water-coolers. ANNE uses a terrible lot of water and that, like the electricity, was something we had to lay on specially. We'd have dried up the local river in a week."

The door of the house had opened suddenly and a man came down the steps to greet them. Dick Maxe had the indefinable air of the solid countryman but he wasn't dressed to display his provenance. He wore a well-cut tweed suit and handmade shoes. Russell put him in his early seventies but he looked hale and strong and his step still had spring in it.

He gave Milden a friendly nod and waited and Milden introduced Charles Russell.

Maxe shook hands firmly. "Delighted," he said. "I'm sorry for all the trouble of getting here but since you've got through we have time for a drink."

Judith's flat was on the *piano nobile* and they went up a rather fine staircase to reach it. The living room was comfortably furnished, a woman's room but not aggressively. Russell noticed with an unspoken approval that there were some very good rugs on the parquet floor.

Dick Maxe said as he poured the drinks: "Judith's cooking the lunch. We ordinarily get our food from the Mess and you'd be surprised how well they feed the new army. But Judith likes cooking when she happens to get the time for it. She'll be in in a minute."

In fact it was ten but she came in collectedly. She was wearing a blue-striped kitchen apron which she took off and casually threw on a sofa. Evidently she wasn't obsessed by convention. Her husband made the introduction and poured her a glass of Campari soda. She sat down and sipped it, very much *dans ses meubles*. "A quarter of an hour to lunch. Dick, will you fix the other drinks." Her English was entirely accentless.

The meal was good and handled efficiently, the helpings served in the kitchen and brought straight in. No fuss with "Do you take this?" You did or if you didn't you left it. The hostess was not a slave; she had time to talk.

Russell watched her as she chatted to Milden. She was Jewish all right but not sensationally; she was slim and rather tall for her race. Russell put her in the last of her forties. She was exchanging professional gossip with Milden, not needing to entertain Charles Russell nor trying, as many women might feel they must, to change his conversation with Maxe to some subject which included themselves.

For Russell and Dick Maxe were getting on well. They had discovered a common interest in birds. Charles Russell was no more than interested but Maxe belonged to a Royal Society and Russell had noticed the puzzling two-facedness which bird-lovers often seemed to display. They would go to enormous pains and expense to preserve some rare species from total extinction but if another were "game" they would shoot it without a pang. So hoopoes weren't quite unknown in Norfolk and a pair had been seen on Maxe's land. With any sort of luck they'd nest there, where they'd be very much safer than three fields away on the land of one of the local magnates who didn't know a hoopoe from a crow. On the other hand the starlings, this year, had been even more of a pest than usual. Maxe had had to dynamite their roosting trees and the slaughter had been satisfactory. But then, of course, a starling was vermin.

For coffee they went back to the living room and Judith asked Russell: "Now what can I tell you?"

"Nothing, thank you. For one thing I'd be out of order if I suggested you tell me some professional secret. And for another I wouldn't understand a word."

Judith Maxe laughed. It was clear and decisive, not a social convenience to change the subject. "Then what can I *show* you? Perhaps the laboratories?"

"No, thank you again. They would tell me nothing."

"Then the bunker. We're rather proud of our bunker. It's heatproof for six hours. Or we hope it is."

"I've been in too many bunkers already."

She looked at him levelly but clearly puzzled. "You couldn't have come here just to check the security. A junior could have done that equally well." She was suddenly the boss and formidable. "Why have you come here, Colonel? I must know."

He had expected the question and had decided his answer. "I came here to meet Mrs Judith Maxe."

There were women who would at once have asked why and he gave her many marks that she did not. Instead she said coolly:

"Of whom you approve?"

"Madam, I approve entirely."

"In that case let us have some more coffee before your other duties recall you to London."

. . . A hit and a well-deserved one at that. But delivered like an accomplished swordswoman.

They drove back to London, for the first part in silence, and Charles Russell was glad of the time to think. Judith Maxe had treated her husband with the sort of respectful attention he'd seen before. She might have been his favourite daughter but he was confident that at one time she had been more. There was nothing unusual in that, Russell thought – they were simply more lucky than many others that their marriage was now on a peaceful sea. But her manner with Arthur Milden had interested him. If he'd had to find a word for it that word would have been simply wary. It couldn't have been an easy relationship, the world class scientist nominally subservient to a politician who was a

50

minor Minister. But there'd been more to it than that – much more. Russell's antennae were sharp and accurate: whatever was between them was personal. She needn't have used such impersonal courtesy, he needn't have looked away when she caught his eye. Russell had seen this too before, the slight unease before an observant stranger of man and woman who had once been lovers. He didn't think they were still, they were neither the type. The affair would have been savage and short for the Arthur Mildens weren't clever with women.

Milden broke the silence finally: "What did you make of the set-up?"

"Odd."

"Perhaps it is but it seems to work. As I told you he's an intelligent man and his degree was not from an agricultural college. He doesn't go down to Yeldham and bore her; he doesn't talk farming or birds to Judith."

"There aren't many of that sort left. I liked him."

"And he gives her what all her race craves, a solid and unquestioned background."

"She didn't strike me as being particularly Jewish."

"I think you may be wrong about that. She has none of the music hall characteristics but she's a passionate and devoted Zionist. I've heard she sends Israel a tithe of her salary."

"I can't think why, I really can't. Any other race but Arabs would have pushed Israel into the sea forty years ago. Now it might take a great power to do it."

"Financially they're in a terrible mess and it's the gesture which counts, the total commitment. On the surface she's as cool as an iceberg but underneath she's an emotional woman."

That I can believe, Russell thought.

They had reached London but he had more to ask. That the head of Yeldham was an active Zionist was the most interesting fact he had learnt that day. "Can you lunch with me tomorrow?"

"I'm afraid I can't. Lord George is seeing the American ambassador and he's asked me to be present too."

"On Thursday, perhaps?"

"With very great pleasure."

"At my club, then." He named it. "At a quarter to one."

Milden put Russell down at his flat where he washed his hands and sent for a taxi. He directed it to the Security Executive. It was time to read Judith Maxe's file but he didn't believe it would tell him much more than he knew. It would record that Judith Maxe was a Zionist but plenty of prominent people were that and it was unlikely that the file would make much of it.

Charles Russell's instinct was quite to the contrary. He had been wise to meet her before reading her dossier.

A formidable woman indeed.

The tribesman had walked a hundred miles in five days. For one of his race that was nothing remarkable, even through barren and mountainous country, for his legs were undamaged and his courage a lion's. But his left arm was gone, sheared away at the elbow, the stump of it swathed in a festering bandage. He'd been working in his fields, he explained, when a piece of the sun had fallen down on his village. When he'd got to it there'd been nothing left so he'd turned his face east and walked to friends.

Later he told them more in detail but he hadn't wished to live for long.

6

Milden had been more than surprised when Lord George, Her Majesty's Secretary of State for Foreign and Commonwealth Affairs, no less, had asked him to attend that morning at his meeting with the American ambassador. He had puzzled over the invitation, finally reaching a private guess: he, Arthur Milden, would be there as a sort of tease, the man who knew the great secret's mysteries and who, if Lord George and His Excellency struck a bargain, could share the latter's car to his embassy and talk to another scientist that same day. Americans were an impatient people and such a bait would be decidedly tempting.

Arthur Milden had laughed for it was no bait at all. Judith Maxe should be attending, not himself. In the end he had accepted happily for the meeting could be more than interesting. Lord George could be extremely tough and His Excellency was a notorious fool.

He was shown to Lord George's splendid room, noticing that the Secretary was alone. The last government had left a single reform which the present one thought it sensible to retain: the Foreign Office had been put in its place, its officials no longer a state within a state. Ministers saw their foreign peers alone.

Lord George rose at once and wished Milden good morning. "I'm sorry I can't offer refreshment. His Excellency might smell it and disapprove. Did you know that amongst his other follies the wretched man is also teetotal?"

"I didn't know that."

"Well, the idiot is." Lord George looked at Milden. "What do you know of him?"

"I know that in his profession he doesn't rate high."

"That puts it with remarkable charity. He's the very worst kind of American envoy. He's enormously rich from a grandfather's piracies and he backed the right party heavily. The pay-off in his case was a major embassy. Not that the Americans now think of us as all that important but the Court of St. James has a certain prestige. Mystique, you could almost call it. Yes, mystique. Anyway, the bloody man's here and we'll have to put up with his numerous defects."

His Excellency was shown in formally and Lord George introduced Arthur Milden smoothly; he did it by giving his name and his office – Minister for Scientific Affairs – watching the ambassador as he named this impressive sounding but in fact minor Ministry. His Excellency was an indifferent poker player and his face showed an instant gratification. This was going to be serious business at last. He sat down and began on his standard sales spiel. He had composed it himself and was fondly proud of it.

. . . Our common heritage of race and language, our unshakable faith in the rule of democracy, our special relationship tested over two wars and beyond . . .

Arthur Milden inspected the ambassador as he droned on. He wore expensive clothes but they were consciously American. If he went to a fancy dress ball, you felt, he would go as Uncle Sam in full fig, stars-and-stripes waistcoat, the whole regalia. Milden mistrusted cardboard cut-outs, especially of figures no longer contemporary, and as he looked at the ambassador and listened he had to blink to believe that this man was real.

He saw that Lord George had been watching the clock and after three minutes he acted decisively, bringing the ambassador down to earth as neatly as he would have shot a pheasant. "I believe we are here to discuss something called ANNE."

His Excellency was offended and showed it; he had a great deal more to say in this vein and he thought it good. But now there was no going back. He hadn't the nerve, as a professional might have, to say blandly: "But we'll come to that later." Instead he looked at Lord George resentfully but nodded a reluctant agreement.

"ANNE has changed the whole balance in Europe." Lord George said it as a deliberate opener.

54

"The tactical balance."

"I accept the correction." Lord George began on his calculated tease. "Of course if you had developed the neutron bomb the advantage would already be yours. But I'm inclined to think you were right not to do so. The Russians were correct for once in calling it a capitalist weapon since it was going to kill men without damaging property." He looked again at the ambassador who was showing irritation increasingly. He was a has-been and thought in a has-been's terms. Lord George was an effete British aristocrat and he was mocking a freeborn American citizen. Rich, too, and that rankled. Wealth was a measure of merit. But of course. "I have sometimes wondered what would have happened in practice. A neutron comes down on a concentration of tanks and the crews know they'll be dead in hours. Do they abandon their tanks and run screaming to mother or do they drive on, dead men but still conscious?" Lord George shook his head. "A macabre reflection."

But His Excellency had had enough. For the first time he uttered words of real meaning. "But we didn't develop the neutron bomb. On the contrary you have developed ANNE."

"Correct," Lord George said.

"We should like it too."

"Of course you would."

"I am here to negotiate."

The ambassador had had his instructions. He himself would have played this long and then longer but his instructions had been precise and urgent. Get this thing ANNE and get it quickly.

"We would naturally offer a *quid pro quo*. I had in mind the matter of your steel. Restrictions would be lifted tomorrow."

Lord George said nothing. The bait was paltry.

"Then some firmer understanding about the Falklands. Argentina will get nasty again."

"We managed the last time."

"Not without our help, you didn't."

"Perfectly true and we're properly grateful, but circumstances have changed since then. I'm afraid that isn't a basis for a deal."

The ambassador swallowed. So it was money they wanted. He'd had instructions on that and had greatly disliked them. He was a close-fisted man and hated parting with money. That this would be his country's, not his own, made no odds. He mentioned a considerable sum.

"Dollars or pounds?"

"In dollars."

"Chickenfeed."

"I could offer half again."

"Without tempting me."

Reluctantly the ambassador went to his limit. "We will double the first figure."

"No deal."

"Then what do you want?" His Excellency was aware that this was bad negotiating; he was now on the defensive, a suppliant. Lord George had outplayed him. He hated this decadent nobleman bitterly but he said again: "Then what do you want?"

"We want Trident."

"But you have it already."

"We want it for nothing and tied up for its useful life."

The ambassador hadn't thought of this and nor had his near-frenzied instructions. It struck him as entirely outrageous. Trident wasn't a single weapon like ANNE but a whole system which would continue over the years. His instinct was to say what he thought but he swallowed again and brought out stiffly: "I shall have to seek instructions on that."

"By all means do so."

Lord George had half risen but His Excellency sat on; he was fighting a private fury and losing but he was still in control though only just. "I feel entitled to co-operation. After all these years of our special relationship –"

Lord George was looking at Arthur Milden. It was an invitation to speak and Milden did. "Not that again," he said. "I beg you."

Understandably the ambassador lost his battle with himself. "We could make it very awkward, you know."

A veil came down on Lord George's patrician face. A peasant was being less than respectful. The days were gone when he could have had him flogged but not the days when he could deal with impertinence. He rose at once. "Good morning, Your Excellency." He started to move to the door to open it but the ambassador had got there first. He opened it for himself and slammed it.

Lord George moved to a corner cabinet. "Horrible little man," he said. "I think we have earned a drink. Let's have one. Sherry or whisky or gin?" he inquired. "I've never got used to gin myself but I don't move upstage when someone else drinks it."

"That's good since I'm the someone else."

"Tonic or bitters?"

"Bitters, please."

Lord George mixed the gin and bitters deftly, pouring a whisky and soda for himself. "Whisky before you have eaten luncheon is supposed to be a mark of depravity. In which case I'm depraved. But I like it."

"The very best reason for drinking it, then."

"You think that too?" Lord George looked at Arthur Milden with interest. He was no longer the very senior Minister talking to one who was much his junior but a man who had struck a spark from another. He asked unexpectedly: "I feel like a natter – care to listen? But I imagine you'll have an engagement for luncheon."

"As it happens I haven't."

"Then lunch with me." He went back to his desk and ordered a taxi. "There's a story that when Gladstone was at Number Ten he had his stationery printed at his own cost. That was carrying it a bit far, I think, and I'm not a man of high moral principle. But I could comfortably walk to my club and I often do. To use an official car as a perk is something which sticks in my old-fashioned gullet." He laughed before he added easily: "You could balance that against the whisky and the way I treated that awful American."

They drove to Lord George's club and went in. It was a convention of recent films and telly that the way to pay a cabby off was grandly to pass him a note and strut away. Lord George, however, did no such things; he waited for his change and tipped reasonably. They sat down for a second and briefer drink and Milden looked around him curiously. He had never been in this club before for it was the temple of the High Tory arcana. There were several men he knew officially and though one or two nodded and smiled at Lord George none of them came up to speak to him. Lord George had noticed Milden's interest and said on a note of the clearest irony: "A bit of a pariah, you see."

"I know I am."

"You misunderstand me. *I'm* the pariah. The members here are the unquestioning faithful and on several points of doctrine I'm unsound. Trident, for instance, but we'll talk at table."

In the dining room Lord George ordered quickly and when the edge of two healthy men's hunger had blunted asked Milden a simple question simply.

"What did you think of this morning?"

"That man's a menace. A pest on top of it."

"Agreed. But I wasn't asking that."

"For the caricature he clearly is I thought you handled him pretty well."

"Thank you, but it wasn't difficult. That sort thinks it's as hard as nails but in practice it's as soft as putty. But any thoughts of your own? On the way it went?"

"I thought you were demanding a lot."

"The Dutch in me, you mean?" Lord George laughed. "Foxy's not ready to trade on ANNE and I knew I wouldn't get Trident for nothing even if I personally wanted it. That's one of the points of doctrine where I'm unsound."

Milden was surprised and asked: "You mean you're against it?"

"No, I didn't say that. But you could call me a very doubtful disciple. The former Prime Minister wanted it badly: it would keep her at the top table, swanning around. But it's difficult to invent a scenario – I think that's the popular word but correct me – it is hard to think of a situation where we'd conceivably dare to use it alone." Lord George finished his carafe of wine; he had ordered two. "Do those wretched Argentinos try tricks again? So we send a Trident-armed submarine and blow up Buenos Aires or Rosario? That is a fantasy of the crudest kind. Or some black dictator starts feeling his oats and locks up his British subjects and tortures them? We're still not so feeble we couldn't react without totally destroying his country. And if it came to a major nuclear exchange any Tridents we had would be pitifully marginal."

Arthur Milden finished his wine in turn. He had heard these views and seen them written – persuasively but not quite convincingly. A prickle of doubt had been left in his mind and was apparently in Lord George's too. If the Cabinet were itself divided . . .

He dared not ask, he was much too junior, and it would be risking a new relationship which he had never expected and now was relishing.

Over coffee Lord George asked: "A brandy?"

Arthur Milden had had one large gin and one small plus a carafe of a generous wine. It was much more than he normally drank at any time. He shook his head.

"I think you are mistaken, my friend." The "my friend" was without the least hint of patronage: it meant simply that Lord George felt friendly. "Alcohol is a drug like another – the proper use of it marks the civilised man. I never try to sink a guest – that's something for first year undergraduates – but since I drink a lot more than you do my opinion isn't wholly worthless. I think you could easily manage a brandy."

"You're doing me very well," Milden said.

"You've just done me a considerable service."

"I can't think what."

"Then I'll have to tell you. You put down that ambassador perfectly. I couldn't have said what you did and lived with it – 'Not that again, I beg of you.' I'm the head of a very touchy Office and though the former Prime Minister slapped the diplomats down they still consider they're something special. Moreover they hang together like insects. If I'd talked like that to one of their corps, the ambassador of a major state, it would have been all over London before the evening. There might even have been a formal protest. Foxy wouldn't have liked that at all." Lord George changed the subject urbanely but firmly. "What do you think of this brandy?"

"It's good."

"It's about the only good thing left in this club. I have another which is much more fun but I brought you here of deliberate purpose." He turned towards Milden and held his eye. "I wanted you to see what you're up against."

"It frightens me."

"Sometimes it frightens me too. It really does."

The porter found them taxis quickly but as Milden was taking his Lord George stopped him. "Would you take it as an impertinence if I offered you a word of advice?"

"Not at all. I'd be grateful."

"Watch Foxy, then. He loathes you. Personally."

"I'd formed the same impression myself."

"I'm sure you had – you're not a fool. But I meant *watch* him, really watch him closely. He could drop you tomorrow but he won't stop at that. If he gets half a chance he'd like to break you."

"I smell as bad as that?"

"To the Foxies you do and he's by no means alone. But to me you smell entirely congenial since we're the same sort of man in all the essentials. The cliché word for me would be aristocrat but I come of a long line of pushful adventurers. Now I'm superficially civilised. You could call me, on a good day, a meritocrat." Lord George smiled amiably. "Just like yourself."

"Then thank you again for luncheon."

"A pleasure."

In the room which was neither round nor square Hair and Wig were looking depressed. On a table between them lay the ambassador's report. Hair tapped it and asked: "What do you think of it?"

"It's gobbledegook."

"Of course it is. He pumps it out as easily as his oil wells pump out crude. In any case one thing's for sure: the British can't have Trident for free. As this idiot for once says sensibly it's not a weapon but a continuing system. If we bound ourselves to give it free we should be binding ourselves to give unconditionally. And we can't afford to do that for a moment. As it is we can fiddle it much as we please. If the British do something we don't approve of we can apologise for late delivery or withhold the essential replacements at will." It was spoken without the least hint of shame. "So it's the only real string we have on the British. So long as they want an independent deterrent, one capable of reaching Russia, it's Trident or nothing and we control Trident. Surrender that and they might opt out. As France has clearly done already."

"Well put."

They fell into reflective silence. They were thinking what was seldom spoken and never, but never, put in writing. Europe was a buffer state which would offer America time to talk before its own cities went up in a nuclear cloud. It was expendable and both men knew it. But buffers must be sufficiently big and with France at the very best uncertain it would be madness to give Great Britain a choice. Both men knew this, as did Hair's other advisers, but Wig had been thinking a little further. "And talking of strings," he said, "there's ANNE."

Hair, who wasn't quick, said at once: "But that isn't a string. We haven't got it."

"Precisely my point."

"Talk straight."

"I will. So long as the British hold ANNE alone they could decide that they didn't want Trident after all. As a battlefield weapon ANNE's enormously powerful. The accepted guess about how war will start is that Russia will move into Europe with armour. But if ANNE were going to make that too costly there wouldn't be any buffer for us. It would have to be first strike or nothing."

"I hadn't thought of that."

"You should."

Hair took a little time to do so; finally he asked uncertainly: "And if Russia had ANNE too?"

"Then the *status quo ante*. The classic attack by massed armour might still be on. That is, if the Russians fired first, as they would. The buffer would still exist but be bloodier. Bloodier and therefore shorter in time."

"Then *we* come out of it badly either way?"

"I'm afraid that's my opinion too."

61

Hair thought that over in total silence. He didn't feel at home with talk like this, abstract appreciations of mights and woulds. He cut the conversation down to a level where he felt more comfortable.

"Then we've got to have ANNE too before it's too late."

Wig didn't think this followed logically but he was much too shrewd to say so openly. And he knew what Hair thought of him: he was suspect. He'd been born in the heartland, in fact in St. Louis, but he'd been sent to an Ivy League college in the East and Easterners weren't Hair's favourite people. Wig knew that Hair would replace him happily if he could do so without upsetting the balance within his court. He asked with a deceptive mildness:

"Then what do you propose?"

"Last time we met I asked you to prepare a plan."

"Which I have done." Wig reached for his briefcase but Hair held his hand up. "You needn't bother, I've made my own. And I've been talking to the Chiefs of Staff."

He was perfectly entitled to do so but Wig listened in a frozen horror. It was going to be an Operation and the capital O scared Wig worse than ANNE. Men would be dropping down from the skies with light artillery and even tanks . . . It was going to be another Iran, a fiasco, a SNAFU. Another and greater humiliation.

Wig asked in a very real astonishment: "And the Chiefs of Staff agreed to that?"

Hair was on his high horse at once. "The business of the Chiefs is to advise. It isn't a part of their duties to agree."

This was strictly correct and Wig conceded it but he said dangerously: "And the politics are for you?"

"So I'm told." For once there was the real rasp of authority.

"You're prepared to accept an act of war?"

"The British won't declare war. They dare not."

"Almost certainly true but they'll withdraw their ambassador."

"Good riddance at that, the man's a dummy. Breaking off diplomatic relations is something which we can easily ride."

"But can we?" Wig said.

"What was that?"

"But can we?" No title of address, just the question.

Hair was furious to be challenged directly but he managed one of his famous smiles. It probably wouldn't work with Wig but it was his reflex escape from any embarrassment. When he felt he had contorted sufficiently he managed to say: "So the State Department tells me. It's sometimes right."

"In one way I agree with you – breaking off diplomatic relations we could ride. It's what the British could still do which would sink us."

"They'd invade Long Island?" It was said for a laugh but raised not the ghost of one.

"Nothing so foolish but they'd act just the same. For the first time in several centuries they'd seek a genuine working alliance with France. And then where would be our buffer Europe? West Germany is not enough."

Hair thought this over for some time. He was capable of the extremes of folly but knew an obstacle when he saw one clearly. Wig saw that he was undecided and for the first time offered a helping hand.

"Would you care to hear my own plan just in case? It is modester but would cause less upheaval."

For the second time Hair held his hand up. "No. Come back in three days when I've considered what you've said."

Which means that he'll talk to his wife, Wig thought, but he left the room with an easier mind. Hair had spoken of time and Wig had been grateful. He didn't approve of rash adventures and the rashest men had been known to cool.

Time was what he wanted most.

7

In the room on the other side of the world, some distance from a burnt-out spyplane, neither man wished to play for time but to reach a result as soon as possible. The atmosphere was one of urgency but the two functionaries were talking amicably. Neither had reason to be other than friendly since neither was in the great rat race for power. They didn't need to watch their backs as the big boys fought for power or survival and their carbon copies were found in most Western states. They were men of enormous influence but theoretically of no power whatever. They had reached the top of their respective trees and these trees were sufficiently far apart to preclude any possible sense of rivalry. The system which they served they believed in. They were happy and contented men.

The elder man was telling the younger and his voice had the dull note of disappointment. "That last test they did in Afghanistan was better than the others but not much. It was still nothing like the heat of ANNE and over nothing like the area ANNE covers."

The younger man nodded and the elder went on. "I'm beginning to have my doubts about Harrison. Our scientists have been working on ANNE, as we know that the Americans have been working independently too, and now their tentative conclusion is this: that the basis of ANNE is a single element which is treated in an unusual fashion. But everything we have had from Harrison points the opposite way – to something complex. As an expert in the arts of deception would you say that that had any significance?"

"Possibly. If it has it is a sinister significance."

"Meaning that we've been misled deliberately?"

"That guess cannot be excluded on what you say."

"Then what are we going to do?"

The younger man didn't hurry to answer; he betted by the form book and mostly won. "Our scientists will get this in time and, since you pointed out the fact, the Americans will do so too. But it would be good to get it before them – cut corners. As things stand we can only do that through this Harrison."

"So?"

"So Azimev gives to Harrison what in effect will be an ultimatum. Put in some vulgar terms he's going to say: The real gen or else."

"Isn't that forcing a crisis on?"

"For Harrison it certainly is. If he gives us the real stuff he's dead. It would be far too risky to leave him alive to talk. Or if he gives us what doesn't work again I'd be inclined to share your own suspicion of the material which he's already sent us. In which case he's a double agent. In which case again he's also dead."

The senior official thought in turn. "Very well. Tell Azimev to do as you say. As for how much time to give to Harrison, Azimev can judge that best. As for the rest, make it tough as you please."

In the language which his parents had spoken Azimev's name had been somewhat different but the man who now was known as Azimev was ambitious and meant to go close to the top. He was already a rising *apparatchik* and the warning which had reached him had frightened him . . . He had been handed an exceptional chance and so far the only results had been negative. Produce something positive or face transfer and demotion.

He had gone to see Miles Harrison at once.

Who had not been entirely surprised to see him for, like his enemies, he had seen it clearly. His present situation must inevitably go one of two ways. Either they would decide he was useless and a possible danger if left to talk or they would guess he'd been leading them blindly to nothing, in which case he was a double agent who obviously deserved the fate of all such men. In either case Miles Harrison was dead.

Nevertheless he had hoped for more time since he hadn't

been feeding Azimev rubbish but the solid and credible latest news on a subject which was exciting most scientists, the behaviour of substances, mostly alloys, when enormous electrical charges were passed through them. Some men suspected that this delayed metal fatigue: others believed the exact reverse. In any case it was a respectable subject and respectable scientists were busy researching it. It was relevant to what went on at Yeldham to the extent of the shocking amounts of energy which Yeldham burnt up in its work on ANNE, but Rhysium wasn't an alloy or metal. It was an artificial man-made element, in fact a highly unstable liquid. When things went inexplicably right you got ANNE. When they didn't you got some useless residue, or quite possibly you burnt Yeldham to ashes. Which made working there extremely interesting.

But when Azimev called at his house again Miles Harrison knew before Azimev spoke that he'd reached his end. He hadn't seen him since he'd first made contact but had been feeding his drop at nicely-spaced intervals. There hadn't been any comment on what he'd sent.

Azimev hadn't blustered or threatened: on the contrary he'd been notably reasonable . . . Harrison had been sending most interesting material and Russian scientists had not been idle. It was a fact that these unheard of charges could produce unheard of internal changes and in one or two cases they'd produced an incendiary. But it was of nothing like the power of ANNE.

Asimev's manner had suddenly hardened. He was still polite and he didn't threaten but he put his demand with naked clarity. On what substance, be it compound or otherwise, was Yeldham currently working to get its ANNE? He would give Harrison just a week to tell him. If he didn't know he would have to find out.

When Azimev left Miles Harrison sighed. He had expected this and had made his plan. Or rather, he thought grimly, his non-plan. He could go to Charles Russell who no doubt would do the orthodox thing; he would hide him till the heat was over. But that might not be for a very long time and away from his work and his relaxations he'd be the shell of a man, a breathing corpse.

He would much prefer to be a real one. He had no children to whom he owed thought or care and his wife, whom in his own way he loved, would have his pension and could teach as well.

He sat down and idly switched on the radio. It was a Labour Shadow Minister addressing a crowd of the faithful. Normally he was fond of classical music but tonight he needed a solid belly laugh and like many of his kind his humour was black. It came out with its own authentic banality, the "I say agains", the repetitive oratory. There were the generalised pleas to mankind as it never was, the more specialised pleas to a half-cloned audience which accepted the cheap act of this windbag only lest worse should befall its policies. Reality was the worst ill of all and so long as this mountebank mouthed and gestured reality could be safely ignored. It was a dish which the faithful lapped up with appetite and a certain Celtic grossness helped it down.

At the end, when the audience woke, there was applause, what was currently called a standing ovation. But Miles Harrison had had his laugh; he turned off the radio and went to bed. He kept a pistol under his pillow now but not with any idea of defending himself. If one attack failed the next would not. He would rather be dead than a motiveless hulk but immediate death might not suit his enemies if they thought he was a double agent who still possessed the real information.

Miles Harrison would have none of that.

When the end came it came as he'd always wished it, quick and decisive and utterly final. He slept lightly and heard the key in the frontdoor lock. Well prepared, he had thought, but that he'd expected. He always slept with a very small night-light, a legacy of an unhappy childhood. A psychiatrist, he had often suspected, would make a tremendous meal of that but in its glimmer he saw two men come through the door. One shone a torch in his face which blinded him, the other swore softly and pulled a pistol. But Harrison had fired first and finally.

8

It had been a very bad twenty-four hours for Milden as he walked home from the gymnasium where he kept fit. It had started the night before with his daughter who had called without appointment when he was tired. He had thought that she had noticeably slipped; she was nineteen but she now looked a decade older and she hadn't been in an agreeable temper. Last time they'd met had been less than successful but there'd been an instant of unexpected sympathy when she'd asked him why he didn't resign from a Cabinet which mistrusted his views and he'd replied that it was sheer bloodymindedness.

But this time there hadn't been even that, for Peggy had been in a mood he detested, one of those flashes of pointless aggression which had sometimes made her mother intolerable when she hadn't been simply vague and feckless. It appeared she had left her steady boyfriend, or perhaps it was the other way round, and was living with a married man who had abandoned his wife and a regular job and who now spent more time on demonstrations (for which he drew a regular fee) than he did in trying to find normal work. She now needed money and had asked for it openly; and the asking had been close to demand. The world owed her a living.

Her father rather thought it did not.

He had given her her money reluctantly, conscious that in a sense this was weakness, more conscious that if he didn't do so she'd slip lower still in a world he detested. He had failed her mother, was failing her too. The least he could do was to see that she didn't want.

And when she had got her money she'd taunted him. She had sometimes come close to that before and he knew that she despised his opinions but this time it was open mockery

. . . The recent Immigration Acts had been an outrage in a civilised country, naked racism disguised as a necessary control, and as for the proposal – yes, she had heard of it – to form a squad to deal with rioting, it would turn the country into a ruthless police state. Openly instead of secretly as it was now. He had listened in a frustrated fury but silently since he dared not argue. He had let it go too far; he had failed. There were excuses, perhaps, like her mother's bad blood but he couldn't escape the fact of fatherhood.

When she left at last he sighed and went to bed but he tossed and sweated miserably, pursued by a recurring thought. No, he wasn't very good with women . . . Peggy's mother and that Russian girl, Judith Maxe, and now his only daughter. As he finally fell asleep at dawn he remembered what he had always known, that he wasn't really interested in the worlds which made a woman's life. But plenty of other men were that and contrived to live with a woman happily. So perhaps, he concluded in a moment of cynicism, it wasn't so much that he wasn't interested as the fact that at home he didn't pretend to be.

And in the morning, still sleeping, there'd been a call from Judith Maxe. Miles Harrison had committed suicide. There hadn't been an inquest yet but the police were not suspecting foul play. A full report would be sent up later but as the master of the Yeldham establishment Judith had thought he should know at once.

. . . But why should Miles Harrison take his life?

A cool voice had said: "That sort often do. I expect he was being blackmailed. They usually are."

Milden had met Harrison twice and had noticed nothing unusual of any kind. He had borne himself like a normal male with none of the traditional signs which were supposed, unreliably, to betray the pederast. But a woman would infallibly spot one. After all it was unfair competition and therefore a matter for women's malice.

He thought Judith's manner excessively impersonal and said curtly: "I'll await the report."

"As soon as possible." She rang off.

He frowned for he hadn't liked what she'd told him and

even less the way she had done it. They'd been colleagues working together closely, you would have thought . . . And you'd have been wholly wrong. He had known there were two sides to her nature and this was one which raised his hackles.

He got up a little later, hot and stale, and his eye fell on the crossed swords on the wall. They were Turkish with bronze hilts, superbly chased, and had been in his family for over a century. By now they were very much part of the furniture but this morning they had conveyed a message, a hint of a warning and much of a real regret. They had come from the Crimean War where they'd been captured from a Turk by a Russian, an RSM who had kept them proudly. Later when the British had captured him he had refused to yield this splendid booty to anyone of lesser rank and Milden's great-grandfather, another Warrant Officer One, had been summoned to accept their surrender. The rules about battlefield booty then had been more generous than they were today and here the swords were on Arthur Milden's wall.

And looking at him, he thought, with a certain reproach. The Mildens had come some way since then, from Sergeant Major to middle rank officer, winning promotion by solid merit. Some men would call it stolid merit in the sort of regiment which made few headlines but took the casualties and won the battles. Son had succeeded father unquestioningly till Arthur had broken the chain deliberately.

Deliberately but had it been wisely? It was the sort of question which Milden mistrusted. All he knew was that he had cut his roots and roots gave a man strength and the calm caution which he knew he lacked.

He went to the morning's Cabinet meeting aware he was going to do something foolish, perhaps earn himself a further humiliation. The meeting would be an important one and, though not of formal Cabinet rank, some junior Ministers had been summoned too. The subject to be discussed was controversial, what Peggy had sneered at the night before, the matter of special police to deal with riots. It had been a favourite with the previous Prime Minister who had been Arthur Milden's effective patron and the planning had been far advanced when she had lost her battle with Foxy and fallen. Foxy's followers had been much less keen and the plan was now on the lap of the gods.

But as he went into the Cabinet room Milden sensed that it was in no such place. It had already been decided – drop it. One or two from the High Tory shires might support it from an unthinking instinct that the peasantry was out of hand, and when many of these peasants were coloured that made the situation more dangerous. But the men from the industrial seats, the Ministers without cast iron majorities, would see it as a threat to themselves. Water cannon? Tear gas? Baton charges? In effect a gendarmerie. But that was wildly un-British, they weren't living in France. Moreover this was an innovation and a taste for ruthless innovations had been what had destroyed the previous Prime Minister.

Nevertheless there had been some support – the situation was undeniably serious – till the Very Senior Legal Figure had spoken in his ageing majesty. For once he wasn't half asleep, no dribble of saliva disfigured his chin. He spoke powerfully and at moments movingly in the manner of the Senior Common Room. The Police must be reinforced and better trained, powers to punish must be increased where necessary, but anything which even smelt of a para-military police was unthinkable. It would be turning our backs on all our traditions, reducing ourselves to a continental level which we despised . . . "The only answer to terror is absolute terror." Who had said that? The old man paused in his moment of triumph. Stalin. And did we want that?

He had sat down in his moment of facile success.

There'd been some further discussion, the tone *diminuendo*, till the Prime Minister looked directly at Milden. He had scented that this was a calculated trap, he had caught a warning glance from Lord George, but he felt strongly and his daemon drove him. He said what he had to without pulling his punches.

He hadn't finished when the Prime Minister said: "Thank you."

He went back to his office and cleared his desk. There wasn't a great deal of paper on it for Milden had been a business man and the first rule of successful business was to know how to delegate work. He wondered how he should spend his evening. He hadn't any formal engagement and he hadn't collected many friends, certainly not the sort of friends whom he could call on without notice and feel at home. He still felt stale and the second snub rankled, and he decided that he needed exercise. He'd go down to his gymnasium and work out his rancour in honest sweat. He had outgrown the muscular Christianity of his brutish little public school but there was nothing quite like violent exercise to purge the human frame of frustration.

And violent it would certainly be since "gymnasium" described indifferently the establishment where he took his exercise. There were none of the old and boring trappings, no bars along the walls and dangling ropes; nor was it one of those modern Keep Fit clubs with their machines for lifting weights on pulleys which doctors insisted could damage the vertebrae. Basically it was for straight karate but had recently moved into fields less formalised. For women were coming in increasingly asking how to protect themselves against muggings and, more recently, rape. This unorthodox establishment had recently begun to do well.

Arthur Milden had always liked it, even in its seedier days. It was kept by an ex-Corporal of Horse who, when he'd tired of excessive bull and ceremony, had transferred to the Physical Training Corps where he'd specialised in unarmed combat. This he still taught with great discretion and only to people like Arthur Milden. He was a responsible man with a social conscience; he wasn't going to produce better thugs however much money was offered to do so.

Unarmed combat had appealed to Milden since it perfectly suited the way he thought. He liked to get down to fundamentals which was the principal reason Foxy mistrusted him and fundamentals weren't confined to politics. Karate could be sufficiently tough but it was still a formalised sport with formalised rules. But what did you do against a man with a bayonet when he'd caught you at stool without your sidearms? Or a thief who carried a knife or a gun? Or in terms of what Milden had sometimes dreamed, what did you do in a burning aircraft when other men were fighting to get out? All normal rules were suspended so . . .

The techniques of this art were not easy to practise without damaging the eager learner but the ex-Corporal of Horse had great experience and Arthur Milden was no longer a learner.

So he went to his unusual gymnasium and rid himself of the worst of resentment. In its early days it had been close to squalid, the changing room small and not always clean, the only way to wash a basin. But now in its deserved prosperity there were hot showers and as many clean towels as you wanted. Arthur Milden took a shower and walked home. He didn't often drink but he would tonight.

He was agreeably tired and by now relaxed and at first the incident failed to register. An elderly woman was walking in front of him, and although where Milden lived wasn't grand it hadn't yet become a ghetto. You didn't look at an elderly woman alone and immediately think of physical danger.

Till it happened and for a second froze you. One mugger had snatched the woman's bag, the other had a club and was beating her down.

She fell in the gutter as Milden reached them. The first man had dropped the bag and was holding a knife. He snarled and said "Keep off" as Milden closed. The knife came up in a right hand sweep and Arthur Milden blocked it as he'd been taught. But he was tired and a little slow in his reflex and he felt the knife bite his forearm savagely. It hurt but it didn't destroy his rhythm. He had slowed the thrust, though he hadn't quite blocked it, and his right hand had caught the attacker's wrist. The man was off balance from his own thrust upwards and Milden let the arm go through, helping it higher, moving very slightly closer. Then he swung the arm smoothly down and backwards, twisting it as he did so, holding the turn. It was the classic Glasgow handshake refined and it dislocated the first man's shoulder. The second clubbed Milden down from behind. The old woman in the gutter moaned on.

Arthur Milden had recovered consciousness in a bed which he could see was a hospital's. A coloured doctor was bending over him but as he opened his eyes he smiled and slipped away. He was well qualified but an Indian and he knew that the man in the bed was important. He doctored by the book of rules and in this case the rules called for Someone More Senior.

He came back in five minutes with a man his own opposite, hearty and brash and a stone overweight. "Good morning," he said briskly.

"Where am I?"

The ex-Rugby football forward said: "Hospital. The Molyneux as it happens. A good one." It was one of the very small ones surviving. "We specialise in all things tropical but we were nearest to where the ambulance picked you up."

Milden's head ached but life was coming back slowly and in any case the doctor was barking again. "You've been concussed but there's no permanent damage. Your left arm was badly cut but we've stitched it up. By the way my name is Waller-Smith." He didn't trouble to introduce the Indian but the Indian smiled at Milden shyly. Milden smiled back; he preferred his manners.

"How long am I going to be here?"

"That depends on how your arm heals. Your head's all right."

"I shan't be out tomorrow?"

"Certainly not. Now sleep a bit more, you're still sedated, and after that we'll think about something to eat." He gave a brusque order to the Indian and stumped off.

Milden slipped into a dreamless sleep. He was still, as the doctor had said, sedated, but a tiny annoyance disturbed his beatitude. He was going to miss his lunch with Charles Russell and that he'd been looking forward to eagerly.

Nevertheless when he woke he laughed. As soon as the doctors would let it do so the Press would be round his bed in force. He would play it as a throwaway and they'd know how to make the most of that. In his mind he saw the blatant headline, MINISTER SAVES OLD LADY FROM MUGGING.

Foxy wasn't going to like that – not at all.

Then Foxy could do the other thing painfully.

9

Earlier in the evening of Arthur Milden's violent encounter the Prime Minister had sent for Charles Russell and Russell had obediently gone to him. He had expected to find him alone, as he was, for only he and Foxy himself had been privy to Harrison's contact with Azimev. Foxy offered refreshment but Russell declined.

"It's Harrison of course," Foxy said.

"It's lucky it was apparently suicide."

"The inquest will find that?"

"I think so. There wasn't the slightest sign of a struggle and no trace of anyone else being present. That doesn't exclude that there was but they'd know their job. Certainly they left no cards."

"Then why did Harrison do it?"

"I think we must assume the Russians became suspicious and impatient. So they put increasing pressure on Harrison who, in passing, was a very brave man. I remember in the war . . ."

Russell stopped. He remembered in the war very well. The young married men had sometimes flinched. Understandably, and few had blamed them, but the Harrisons had owned their own lives. No children tugged at their sleeves, no women clacked.

The Prime Minister hadn't picked him up and Russell went on in the present firmly. "He could have come to me and of course I'd have hidden him but he wouldn't have liked a life in hiding and his disappearance would have been politically awkward. He was a considerate man as well as a brave one. And the other sort of disappearance, a snatch by the Russians and having it wrung from him, was something which he sensibly wouldn't face."

"We've been lucky," Foxy said.

"We have. The newspapers may be curious since we can't hope to hide where Harrison worked and they'll soon find out how he spent his spare time, but there won't be a strong lead to Intelligence and they'll probably drop it fast as the usual thing – man of unorthodox habits blackmailed too hard."

"Then what's going to happen now?"

"I don't know. I expect the Russians will try again but on the form book they'll do nothing foolish. They'll try the same thing which is loosely called spying; they'll pick on somebody else and work on him."

"Not through Azimev they won't."

"I'm delighted to hear you say it."

"I do." The Prime Minister sounded entirely confident. The last Prime Minister had had several defects but the Foreign Office had been effectively tamed. Diplomats were now civil servants and when told to do a thing they jumped. If the Prime Minister expressed a wish that a certain quasi-diplomat leave the country he left double quick without argument. "Then I'll ask Lord George to act at once but I won't tell him what you've just told me. There are adequate grounds to get rid of Azimev."

Charles Russell started to rise but Foxy checked him.

"So you think the Russians may try again but that they'll do so within the accepted rules?"

"That's my guess."

"I agree with it. But the Americans are another animal."

"One capable of dangerous action."

"Then shouldn't we increase security?"

"At Yeldham? I thought it pretty tight already. And if the Americans did decide on some madness we could station a division there without making any practical difference."

"Just the same –"

"I will see to it."

The Prime Minister offered refreshment again and this time Russell accepted gladly. "America –" he said.

"It frightens you?"

"It scares me stiff."

"Anything concrete to go on?"

"Nothing. Only an instinct that something is cooking."

"If there is I'm afraid it may cook pretty fast. Lord George has another meeting tomorrow. Not with the ambassador – he's diplomatically sick – but with his senior official who's a high class professional. And Lord George will stick to his guns. I told him to." The Prime Minister rose. "That seems to be all for the moment. And thank you."

Charles Russell went to his supper thoughtfully. It was the waiting game again and he'd play it but there was something which he hadn't told Foxy since it was far too vague for clear discussion. On the face of it the dangers were Russia and America but Russell had a hunch and would run it.

Miles Harrison had been rather unlucky for he hadn't been a committed man. But Russell had recently met a woman who was. A woman at Yeldham, Judith Maxe. Judith Maxe was a committed Zionist.

He liked to grasp his nettles firmly and rang up Judith Maxe after supper. When they'd met before she had snubbed him briskly and he expected a certain chill of manner. Instead she was relaxed, even friendly. "I was expecting you to call," she told him.

He was surprised and said on a reflex: "Yes?"

"I've been positively vetted before."

"Positive vetting is not my business. I am ringing to ask you to lunch when it suits you."

It was her turn to be surprised; she asked: "Why?"

"The pleasure of your company."

"Oh."

"And a little official business on the side."

"I wondered why you'd come to Yeldham. Unless you had some science secretly the place could have told you nothing whatever."

"I don't have any such secret knowledge."

"Then why did you come?"

"I came to meet you."

"And the meeting was unsatisfactory?"

"Not unsatisfactory, simply inadequate." She was fencing with him and Russell knew it. He was suddenly briskly male

77

and compelling. "Now are you coming to lunch or are you not?"

He heard her laugh and the sound was agreeable. "You interest me, you really do. You have a shocking reputation with women."

"Thank you very much indeed."

"I will lunch with you with the greatest pleasure."

He pressed his luck. "Tomorrow, then?"

"I have an engagement tomorrow." A pause. "I will break it."

"At half past twelve?"

"I'm a punctual woman."

He had named a restaurant which was fashionable in a solid and unfussy way and where the food was also good and unfussy. In this year of grace they were not all that easy to find. He arrived at a quarter to twelve and sat down in the bar, rising when she came in, precisely on time. He had noticed what she had drunk at Yeldham and suggested Campari confidently.

"You're very observant."

"I'm paid to be so."

He watched her as she drank the Campari. It wasn't the sort of restaurant where a world-class physicist would be instantly recognised, nor did Judith Maxe in the least resemble one. She looked like a woman of taste and means and Russell fancied that her short fur was sable. She would avoid the vulgarity of a theatrical mink. Privately he purred contentedly. He liked to be seen with elegant women.

The head waiter arrived to take their order, handing them both an impressive menu. Judith put hers down without a glance. "One of the pleasures of eating with men is that they sometimes know more about food than women."

"You would like me to order for you?"

"I insist."

They finished their aperitifs comfortably and the head waiter came back to escort them in. She nodded at the whitebait, pleased. "You can't get these at Yeldham."

"So I supposed. But it was a gamble that you would like them."

"Which you win."

He watched her again as she ate with appetite. She might be a world-ranking scientist but she was also very much a woman. Her manner with the head waiter himself had been that of a woman well used to head waiters but in serving the whitebait a waitress had dropped a fork and for an instant Judith Maxe had frowned. Russell had seen it and made a mental note. She wasn't a civil service battle-axe: a man could work with her perfectly happily. But not, he rather fancied, another woman. The malice of women to other women was incalculable. This was a happily female animal.

When the jugged hare arrived she nodded again. "Clever of you," she said.

"And lucky. There are women who can't bear to face it."

"I'm not one of them." She was eating with gusto still, taking the edge off a healthy appetite. Halfway through the hare she said: "Now tell me what all this is about."

"To begin with it's about ANNE itself and then about the political background."

"That's two separate subjects – I'll take ANNE first. I don't want to sound in the least superior but there is nothing I could tell you of ANNE which you would understand or I might tell."

"I think there is."

"All right. Go on."

Charles Russell who had been briefed said carefully: "Of the many attempts to make ANNE some have failed. A few, in fact, came close to disaster. But in those which succeeded you were almost always in charge."

"And what do you make of that?"

"A coincidence."

She looked at him with a new expression: for the first time there was a gleam of hostility. "Some woman's art or some woman's flair like putting a little fennel in pea soup?"

He returned smoothly to the matter in hand. "ANNE seems to go beyond orthodox physics, the sort of thing you can put in equations. It's untidy and most unscientific. So I wondered if you were holding something back."

She took it without a blink. "That's perfectly legitimate reasoning. But tell me why I should hold something back."

"That's the second part of the question I asked you, the politics behind this horrible ANNE."

"I don't think I follow."

"It's perfectly simple. It's known you are a committed Zionist."

"And so might give Israel my hypothetical secret?"

"To use your own phrase that's legitimate reasoning."

She put down her knife and fork to answer. "I haven't," she said, "and I don't intend to." She looked at him straitly, weighing him carefully; finally she said: "But I might. There are circumstances in which I'd put Israel first."

"That," Russell said, "is frank. I thank you."

"But they're very unlikely indeed to arise. We're enormously better soldiers still and America gives us an edge in technology. But that cannot make us equal in manpower. We can't take serious casualties and the Arabs can. In the unheard of event that they for once got together they could put us with our backs to the sea. In which case you know very well what would happen. Revenge is in our blood as it isn't in yours. The Arab capitals would be rubble as we drowned. Whether we have the Thing assembled is something I neither know nor wish to but I'm assuming, as I expect you do too, that in a crisis we could make the Big Bang."

It was an opinion widely held on good evidence and Russell didn't waste time in denying it. "Then if you've got the Thing itself why bother with poor relation ANNE?"

"Because to blow up the Arab capitals would be unpopular internationally and still leave us on our beaches defeated. But ANNE destroys masses of men and armour too. We shouldn't have been driven to the sea."

"Logical again," Russell said.

"I have a weakness for intelligent reasoning. That's why I'm talking unwisely to you."

"I don't think it's as unwise as all that. Abetting a treason is not my business but nor is it any part of my duty to write minutes on a mere hypothesis." Russell spread his hands in deliberate vagueness. "If there's a secret in ANNE within a secret, if certain events occurred in the Middle East . . ."

"I haven't admitted there is such a secret."

"Nor have you denied it."

"True. You haven't asked. If you did I should. You were right in thinking I'm wholly committed."

He watched her again as she finished the jugged hare. She was a striking woman at any time but now glowed with a sudden intense vitality. Charles Russell felt the power of it physically. As dangerous, he thought uneasily, as the ANNE which she controlled. If she did.

Or maybe did not – he wasn't going to find out by asking. It was time to bring the tension down so he looked at her empty plate. "A little cheese?"

"I've eaten too much already, thank you."

"Coffee, then? And a glass of Armagnac?"

"I'd like that very much indeed."

Over them she began to relax, her momentary excitement spent. She was again the faintly wary scientist, conscious of Charles Russell's profession.

He took his cue from her and said lightly: "So I'm lunching with a potential traitress. As a matter of professional interest how would you smuggle your secret out?"

She saw at once that this was a game again: emotion had died, they were fencing conventionally. "If it's the sort of secret you seem to think it I could hardly get it out in writing, not even in the equations you mentioned. I'd have to go myself."

"You'd be stopped."

"I *have* been stopped and I much resented it. It appears that in my contract of service there's a clause that I may not leave the country without asking some official first. I was going on a simple holiday, to Bermuda as it happened, with a man. And stopped we were at London airport. Very polite, but they stopped us. As I said, I very greatly resented it."

"I don't see why."

"It suggested suspicion."

"Not necessarily of yourself, you know. You were and are a very valuable property. It was reasonable to ask for time to make arrangements for your protection abroad. Suppose you'd been snatched and they'd beaten it out of you."

"In Bermuda?"

"Why not? Whatever sort of man you went with."

She looked at him with rekindled interest. "You are interested in my private life?" Again there was a bite of acidity.

"Private lives are part of public persons." It was pacific and intended to be so.

It worked. "Yes, I suppose they are. And I'll tell you something else, Colonel Russell. You're an exceptionally intelligent man. I watched you when you came down to Yeldham. You were watching Arthur Milden and myself – what we said to each other and what we didn't. I think you knew we had once been lovers. That's why I was as rude to you as I was. Women don't care for men who notice too much."

"I wasn't being vulgarly curious.'

"Now I've met you I'm perfectly sure you weren't and I'd like you to know that I'm not an adventuress. I had British nationality two years before I married Dick Maxe and though he was comfortably off I was well enough paid. He was much older than I was but it was real while it lasted. Now I must take an occasional lover but I do so with the greatest discretion. Adultery is just a word but shaming a man you have loved is a crime."

It wasn't so far from his own philosophy and it suited this elegant woman well. Russell could see she was still relaxing; she was feeling the need to talk and he let her. He'd been a formidable interrogator but also had the arts of a good priest. At sympathetic silence he excelled.

She broke it as he had hoped she would by returning to her affair with Milden. "Arthur," she was saying reflectively, "was something of a one-off job." She quoted a snatch from a Cole Porter lyric, smiling a little wryly, regretful.

A trip to the moon on gossamer wings
Just one of those things.

"That wasn't my normal form at all. I like a man to have roots and feel their pull. As my husband has and always will have. It makes me feel secure and I need to. Arthur has cut his roots deliberately."

82

"I wouldn't be too sure of that."

Russell knew that this was an understatement. No man could wholly escape his backgound, his genes if you accepted that term . . . Those generations of unpretentious service in regiments which had never been fashionable, the values which they had imposed inescapably . . . Arthur Milden had come a long way from those. Russell's private assessment echoed Lord George's. Arthur Milden was a successful meritocrat. But put him in a situation which spelt out to him the ancestral word duty and Milden wouldn't think of his career. He would quietly do what he felt he must. Yes, felt for once, not simply calculated. And if that action broke or killed him then that again would be one of those things.

Russell noticed that Judith Maxe had looked at her watch. She had seen him do it and held out her wrist. "Dick gave me that," she said, "on our honeymoon. I've never worn another and never shall. Thank you for a lovely lunch and for listening to a load of rubbish."

"I didn't think it rubbish."

"Maybe. You're a dangerously clever man and you have charm to make it even more dangerous. Come down to Yeldham whenever you fancy. Just give me a ring and I'll fix something to eat."

"I'd like to do that," Russell said.

He meant it. Judith was another meritocrat. They weren't his clan but he was beginning to like them.

Lord George had done as Foxy had asked him and arranged to see the senior diplomat at a time a little later that morning. He liked him as he despised the ambassador and the interview would not be tedious – no boring lectures on common heritage, no appeals to cultural background which didn't exist. Meanwhile there was an awkward file and he frowned as he read the minutes unhappily.

A Russian quasi-diplomat had been caught in undiplomatic activity and Security wanted him out of the country. Moreover the Prime Minister was backing the proposal strongly. That decided the matter but not the timing. It wasn't so very long ago that the Foreign Office would have raised every objection, both of fact and as a matter of principle; it would have demanded to see the hardest evidence, for Azimev had been semi-accredited, a part, whatever his nationality, of the sacrosanct *cher collègue* clique which had acquired for itself outrageous privileges and for centuries had defended them stoutly. But the previous Prime Minister had changed all that, challenging it head on and winning, establishing firmly who gave the orders and who obeyed, yet a practical difficulty still remained. Retaliation would be inevitable and Britain might not come out best on the tit for tat. Lord George would have to look into that. A pawn for a pawn would be quite acceptable but if the move cost a bigger piece it was not.

He could easily get rid of Azimev but he couldn't achieve it tomorrow morning.

He telephoned to the Prime Minister, saying so. The Prime Minister took the point but urged all speed . . . How long?

Say a fortnight.

Make it a week.

Lord George dismissed the file reflectively. There was clearly something in this affair which he didn't know. Foxy's intervention was unusually urgent in a matter which was often routine. It was not unreasonable to guess it had been sparked by some report from Intelligence that Azimev was close to ANNE. Lord George thought that Foxy was mishandling ANNE but whichever way he chose to play it he would want to get rid of a spy who might steal his hand.

That wasn't the Foreign Secretary's affair. Get rid of Azimev and they'd send another. They played it by the unwritten rules and always had. But the Americans were another matter and very much a Foreign Secretary's business.

Instinctively he washed his hands before receiving the American diplomat. Lord George knew him well and liked him better. He had risen in his profession by merit, not by making subventions to a political party's funds, and Lord George had a sincere respect for the hardboiled pro who knew his business. Such men were notably easier to deal with than dummies whom their staff propped up loyally.

Nevertheless he wasn't quite happy for he had had his

84

instructions and privately questioned them. They had been that he wasn't to lower his terms and he knew that what he'd been told to insist on would be unacceptable to the other side. Moreover the Prime Minister puzzled him. For a man of his age he tired rather easily but he was reputed to sleep eight hours like a baby. And here he was behaving like a man on a very short rope indeed, playing for the impossible coup before the rope ran out and broke his neck. Lord George would have been happy to negotiate seriously for he knew what he wanted and could probably get it.

Irritating – extremely irritating. Foxy was clearly playing this big and Lord George had grave doubts that he held the chips. He would have agreed with Charles Russell on the habits of scientists: somehow they seemed to keep in step whatever the efforts to keep them apart. Russia would have got the bomb without a stream of traitors to cut the time needed. Russia and America would similarly get ANNE in time. In time. How much time? He didn't know and nor did Foxy. So why not strike a sensible bargain while the counter was still on the table to play with? But Foxy had carried the Cabinet with him and Lord George would go along since he must.

He received his guest formally – formally but with a genuine sympathy. The man was going to offer a bargain and in fact it was extremely generous. In return for immediate know-how on ANNE there'd be a cast iron guarantee of support in a sensitive and otherwise indefensible area. Lord George had suppressed a desire to whistle, for the price of that in domestic politics meant that America was near-desperate for ANNE. He himself would have accepted happily and it went against centuries of family advancement to turn down flat what he saw as profitable.

But at the end he said simply: "I'll have to put that up, you know."

The diplomat understood doublespeak perfectly; he rose and said in turn: "I wish you luck."

He walked to the door, Lord George going with him. At it for a moment he halted. And now, the Foreign Secretary thought – now it will be stick, not carrot.

It came as Lord George had known it would with the

easy perfection of very long practice. The Minister didn't threaten or bluster as his nominal master very well might have. Instead he said in his Ivy League accent: "May I say that you're running a very grave risk."

It was a warning in the most delicate clothing, one which Lord George had expected and felt he deserved. The answer must be equally delicate. To say: "I agree" would be close to disloyalty; to stay silent would be plainly rude and might well be mistaken for upper-class huffiness. Finally Lord George said simply: "Yes."

He returned to his desk more uneasy than ever. The Americans were not good losers, nor did they see the least reason to be so. If they acted they would do so quickly and God alone knew what they'd choose to do.

Charles Russell would have agreed wholeheartedly.

IO

Lord George had been right as he often was and America was acting first. Hair had decided that action was necessary but his wife had weaned him from delusions of grandeur.

So Hair and Wig were raking it over and this time it was Wig who had the edge. He had started with the advantage of a contempt which he had felt was justified: Hair had been talking big but now spoke small. As a State Governor he had dealt firmly with student demos (to the applause of those whose taxes supported them) and privately had convinced himself that he was a man of inflexible will and purpose. In fact he bent to every breeze which ruffled his chances of re-election. Last time he'd spoken with Wig he'd had a plan, a grandiose plan which had frightened Wig badly, and when Wig had pointed out its defects he had conceded nothing but said that he'd think again. Which clearly he had done; he had wavered.

"Last time we spoke we left it in the air." (You mean you got cold feet and held off.) "I'm still determined we've got to have ANNE but I decided to try once again through diplomacy. But those bloody British refuse to play ball."

All this Wig knew though he didn't say so. It would be unfair to say that he spied on his master but he had to know what the man was doing.

Hair switched to a partly justified diatribe on the ungratefulness of Europeans, how they took transatlantic protection for granted but wouldn't get off their bottoms to help. They spent money on bloated social services which should have been spent on conventional weapons. They insisted on independent deterrents which they'd never dare to use independently and would be nothing in a major exchange. They were Nervous Nellies, a pain in the ass.

With most of this Wig agreed entirely but he had heard

87

it too often for other than boredom and he thought that phrases like Nervous Nellies were the mark of a painfully second-class mind. He let Hair run on for a while, then stopped him dead.

"Then what do you now plan to do?"

Hair blinked. He was accustomed to a discreet subservience but Wig, though discreet, was not subservient. It was known that he wasn't unduly ambitious and if you pushed him he would resign at once.

Leaving you to explain to the nation why the head of a controversial body had walked out and was making no public comment. In an election year that would be more than embarrassing.

Hair blinked again but fell back on a tried technique. When asked an awkward question he threw it back. He managed one of his infamous smiles and said to Wig: "Tell me what *you'd* do."

"You asked me to prepare a plan. I have."

"Let's hear it, then."

Wig knew he had won but was also human; he wanted his pound of flesh from a man he despised. "May I take it you have now abandoned the other plan we discussed before?"

"On further consideration . . ." It tailed away.

"Then instead of a body of men I shall drop a man."

"A single man?" It sounded incredulous.

"A single man has as good a chance as a gang of heavily armed desperados. You could drop a division on the Yeldham establishment without achieving more than a state of war. As you said once before the British would duck it but what's left of NATO would fall to pieces. This way there's a chance it won't."

"What happens if this man gets killed or caught?"

"My bet is the British will play it *piano*. They'll protest, of course, but they won't do it publicly. It won't upset the Atlantic Alliance. We shall still have our buffer states in Europe. For whatever you may think they are worth."

"I don't think they're worth a dime myself but there are plenty of people who think they're important."

"I'm one of them myself. They buy time. While their cities go up we can still make signals."

Hair frowned a trifle nervously for this was too close to the truth to hear comfortably; he decided to return to the details. "How are you going to get this man in?"

"He won't be falling out of the skies with a parachute and all the clobber. I'm going to winch him down from a chopper at night."

"If you use a chopper from one of our bases I can't see how you're going to hide it."

"I'm certain we couldn't hide it so I shan't. The chopper will come from one of our ships which will be sailing up the Channel legitimately. In fact to an exercise off Trondheim. Yeldham is forty-five miles inland. An hour later, if he's still alive, our chopper will pick our man up where it dropped him. If he doesn't keep his rendezvous the chopper flies back to its ship without him."

"Security will be pretty tight."

"Security is extremely tight. But there's a lake with an island out in its middle. I think the best bet is to drop him on that."

"With an inflatable?"

"There's a punt on a continuous wire."

Hair rubbed his carefully shaven chin. He didn't like Wig or his East Coast manners but he could recognise good planning – an outside chance; he asked at length: "This man is a scientist?"

"He isn't what you'd call a top-flighter but he knows enough to know what to look for. Assuming he gets near enough to look. And that, before you say it yourself, is going to need a great deal of luck."

"A great deal," Hair said at once. He thought so too.

"But he's been lucky in the past – that's why I chose him. He's a Puerto Rican. Name of Romero and very experienced."

"He's going to need all of it."

"That's a fact."

"And as I said before the luck of the devil."

"He wouldn't like to hear that. He's a pious Catholic."

★

The siren woke Judith Maxe at five o'clock. It was set off as a practice drill twice a month but as head of the establishment she was warned of these occasions and ignored them. She hadn't been warned of this and dressed quickly.

She was puzzled for the timing was wrong. They had started what they called a process at around eleven the previous evening and normally it was at least nine hours before anything of significance happened, before the critical master dial began to climb. They had slipped into using household words for the terrifying forces they played with, so Rhysium was the steak-and-kid and its complicated treatment the cooker. By making rather feeble jokes about matters which secretly scared you stiff you instinctively diminished their terror. There was material here for a psychiatrist's thesis but such creatures weren't thick on the ground at Yeldham.

As she passed her husband's dressing room Judith Maxe looked into it quickly. He had already gone. She smiled – he hadn't cravenly abandoned his lawful wife; he would have taken his gun and gone down to the island where a pair of Canada geese was nesting. The gun wouldn't be for the Canada geese but for the cannibal magpies which stole their eggs.

As she trotted to the bunker's entrance she tried to keep her mind a blank for it was fatal in any matter of science to start guessing before you knew the facts, to make prejudgements which might later cloud your mind. Instead she thought about geese and magpies. Her husband had told her a lot of the latter. To a countryman they were birds of ill omen. Also they were reputed to mate for life. If you saw one alone it was widow or widower and it might somehow project its bad luck on yourself. So you wished it "Good morning, good morning, good morning" which, by centuries of rural wisdom, would somehow avert its power to do you ill. But if you saw two together you needn't bother. They were beautiful beasts but had horrible habits and one might shoot them to protect rarer fowl.

She went down twenty steps to the bunker, rang and was admitted promptly. There were three doors behind her now. She looked around.

She was trying to gauge the mood of the gathering for all crowds soon developed their own personality. At the moment it was sensibly anxious but it wasn't yet a mood of panic.

And there was reason for a real anxiety: the soldiers and MoD police were here and like Judith they were warned of mere drills and didn't come. But barring the perimeter patrol which was judged to be out of the range of danger all were now present and sitting quietly.

Yeldham was wide, wide open to the skies.

But this wasn't what the civilians were thinking. This was a real alarm at last and this bunker had never been put to the real test. They knew there were four feet of concrete above them and they knew that experienced engineers had sworn on their mothers' graves that this would suffice. But experienced engineers could be wrong. For an instant the little crowd stirred collectively and Judith felt it do so sharply. They were sitting in a potential hell in a flameproof capsule which hadn't been proven.

Her Number Two came up to her and led her silently to a bank of instruments. They were relays from the laboratory, duplicates of those which Miles Harrison had once watched with an increasing anxiety. But today there was a frightening difference. The finger on the master dial was already beyond the red line of danger.

"Current off?" Judith asked.

"Of course."

"You're sure?"

"The cut-outs shot twenty minutes ago."

"Then any idea what's going on?"

"None." He corrected himself. "Or rather one." He pointed at the dial in emphasis. "If that cooker is going to blow at all it ought to have blown several points below that."

They were interrupted by one of the sheltering soldiers. He had a radio to an outside aerial and was talking loudly, perhaps a little louder than he would have wished. They heard a voice say:

"Patrol here."

"Receiving you."

"A helicopter has just flown over us."

"Did you see its markings?"

"It's still too dark."

"Very well, I'll report it on. Now Out."

The dial was still climbing slowly, remorselessly. It wasn't visible to the seated staff but Judith could sense that their tension had increased. If they break, she thought, and panic, rush the doors . . . She had seen a mass panic once in her childhood when a crowd had been charged by mounted police in her native land. She herself had escaped but it hadn't been pretty.

Her assistant too had felt the tension rise; he jerked his head at the staff behind them. "Would you care to say a few words?"

"No thank you." She wasn't a professional actress, she couldn't summon the manner of reassurance. They'd smell she was as scared as they were.

The needle was still climbing but more slowly. They sat for another ten minutes in silence.

An MoD man was the first to break. He let something between a scream and a wail and, wailing still, stood up and ran for the doors.

The establishment's staff nurse was on him instantly, grabbing him and slapping his face. He stood for a moment, uncertain and shocked, then said ashamedly: "Thank you. I'm sorry."

Nobody else had had time to move.

The Number Two had touched Judith's shoulder. "It's steadying," he said softly.

She looked. "It is."

"And maybe moving back a bit."

She counted sixty seconds on the watch Dick Maxe had given her; finally she said: "You're right."

She'd felt the terror of the great powers of darkness but now sloughed it with an admirable discipline. She asked casually: "Is it Thursday today?"

"As it happens it is."

"Because Thursday is my lucky day."

II

As it had been lucky for the Puerto Rican Romero who had landed in the heart of Yeldham at a moment when normal security had ceased to exist inside the perimeter fence. That was a good mile away and considered to be outside the danger zone. There were men on it still and one had radio-ed . . . A helicopter had flown over. Noted . . . But within the fence there wasn't a soul above ground.

More accurately there was one, Dick Maxe. He was used to the dark, which was in any case lightening, and though he had a torch used it seldom. He had taken the punt on its endless cable to pull himself across to the island and there he settled in his carefully made hide. Canada geese were wary birds: a canvas screen and some brushwood wouldn't do. You had to dig yourself in and Dick Maxe had done so. The spoil from his little pit was still there, a neat pile which he had covered with branches. The spade which he had used was with it.

He watched the nest through his German nightglasses. At the first real light the gander would fly, foraging for his sitting mate. If the magpies came Maxe would shoot them ruthlessly.

He heard the helicopter before he saw it, puzzled that it should be where it was. Yeldham was a prohibited area – its pilot could be in serious trouble. And it seemed to be hovering over the island. It was first light by now and Dick Maxe looked up.

The chopper was doing more than hover. It was lowering a man on a wire.

Maxe had heard the alarm but had paid no attention; he had taken it for another drill and, though when Judith's guest he obeyed her rules, this was surely a clear case for exception. By the time he had pulled across to the mainland

and walked the half mile to the communal bunker the alert would be over and he'd have wasted his time. He looked up and frowned at the hovering chopper.

The man on the wire was unexplained but one possible explanation frightened Dick Maxe. Collectors of rare eggs were known to be mad. Mad enough perhaps, just perhaps, to hire a helicopter to ravage a nest.

In the growing light he looked again at the helicopter. It was curious that it bore no markings. The man on the wire was still coming down slowly. Christ, he was going to land plumb on the hide.

In the event he did not for he sheered away suddenly. With the light had come the small wind of dawn and it swung the man away to the water. He was only a few feet above it and he let go. The splash disturbed the shy geese. They flew away.

Dick Maxe climbed out of his hide with his shotgun. He had forgotten the magpies but not his weapon. The man was swimming strongly towards the island. Maxe walked towards him, then hid in the undergrowth.

The shore of the island was muddy and treacherous but the stranger pulled himself up by a tree root. He stood there wet as a rat and swore. The accent was very clearly American.

Maxe rose to his feet and walked towards him. Like many big men he trod more lightly than most and at first the man from the wire didn't hear him. When he did he reacted instantly, reaching under his shoulder for his gun. But his sodden clothes slowed his normal draw and Dick Maxe had seen that motion before. He gave the stranger both barrels at six feet range.

He sat down on a log and lit a pipe. The geese had flown so they wouldn't smell him and in any case he'd stopped thinking of the geese. Egg poachers were a contemptible breed but they weren't normally American and he'd never heard of one carrying a pistol.

He turned the body over with his foot, taking the gun from the waterlogged holster. He knew a little of weapons generally but nothing of the one he held. In fact it was Czechoslovakian. Wig was a very careful man.

Dick Maxe sat down again to think it over, thinking slowly but with an admirable clarity. He'd blown most of the stranger's head off at point blank range. The man had tried to draw on him first but if it came to an inquest Maxe couldn't prove it. Besides, before it came to an inquest there'd be every sort of enquiry and trouble. He led a well-ordered life and avoided disturbances. To be hauled into a coroner's court would certainly upset his gentle routine.

What he must do was get rid of the body.

And there was another aspect which grew as he thought of it. If this man were not a poacher of eggs which now seemed something less than probable he was a man of a very different trade and it might suit the mysterious powers which ruled Yeldham if he simply disappeared without trace. He, Dick Maxe, might be wrong about that but they could always dig the bastard up. He'd tell Judith what had happened and leave it to her.

He bent his strong back and hauled the body to his hide. He toppled it in, threw the pistol after it. Then he filled in the hide with the spoil taken from it. He thought for a moment, then took the spade with him.

In the punt he considered cutting the cable but decided there was no point in doing so. The island was patrolled at intervals and if they found the cable cut it would look odd. So let them visit this island freely when they'd find what they were bound to find, a foolish old birdwatcher's hide filled in. The old silly had given it up. So what?

He put the spade back in a shed and went upstairs. The All Clear was sounding as he went to the bathroom. There he stripped to the skin and left his clothes on the floor. The blood on the jacket was stiffening darkly.

He put on fresh clothes and went down to the kitchen where he cooked himself an enormous breakfast. Odd, he thought – very odd indeed. After battle he had always been ravenous. He'd seen messier deaths than that stranger's but few. It was lucky that he wasn't queasy.

He was standing at the stove still as Judith came in. It was typical that she didn't ask him where he'd been.

"That alarm," she said, "was for once the real thing. Be

95

an angel and do me some breakfast too." Normally she didn't eat it. "I was as frightened as a cat with kittens. Fear makes me hungry."

"Yes, I know. I've just killed a man. That makes *me* hungry."

"You're joking, of course."

"I'm afraid I'm not. Let me finish the breakfast – we'll talk at table."

He brought it to her and told his story. "I must think," she said and was silent to do so. Finally she said: "I'm proud of you."

"Firing first, you mean? That was a reflex. I've been drawn on before – in the war, it was. The man concerned was a German officer and he didn't carry his gun in a shoulder holster. But the movement is much the same at the start."

"You told me you got a gong in the war."

He laughed at that. "I believe I did."

"Anyway I love you dearly."

"That's very nice indeed to hear. I might impose on you a little later. Just at the moment we must make a decision." He hesitated but brought it out. "If that American was what we both seem to be guessing why did they send a single man?"

She said very much what Wig had told Hair. "Drop a dozen and they'd be all over the place. One of them would get spotted for certain and Yeldham would be a wasps' nest in no time. They thought a single man had a better chance."

"It's arguable," he said.

"I'd have argued it."

"Then what are you going to do?"

"Tell Colonel Charles Russell."

"The Russell Arthur Milden brought here for lunch? I was impressed by him."

"You are not alone. He has since entertained me back. I enjoyed it."

"That was nice of him," Judith's husband said. His expression hadn't changed as he said it. His wife had friends in high places and he had not. "And what would you guess he's going to do?"

"Tell me what you'd do."

"I?" He laughed again. "Who am I to think for the great and the powerful?"

"In your way you're a whole lot shrewder than most of them."

"Then I'd do most things to avoid an incident. This isn't a moment to annoy the Americans. I'd be tempted to do nothing whatever."

"Charles Russell will be tempted too."

"Then he's a sensible man as well as congenial. I suggest you ring him up at once. I believe you have a security blower. And when you come back I've a favour to ask of you, the gross imposition I mentioned before."

"Why not ask it now?"

"Very well, I will." He pushed his plate away from him firmly. "In the bathroom is a set of my clothes. They're soaked with that American's blood. In detective stories the criminal burns them but the great detective finds the traces."

"The great detective won't find this lot. There are advantages in a private laboratory."

"That's really very obliging indeed but perhaps you ought to telephone first. I'll stay here and keep an eye on the bathroom."

"Of course you're right." But she rose reluctantly. There was something she wanted to say but she'd startle him. She had said: "I love you dearly" but casually. Now she wanted to turn the years back and say it again.

She frowned as she walked to the security telephone. It was a frown of bitter disgust at herself. I'm a female four-letter man, she thought, but at least I've been extremely discreet. Dick might have guessed – he knew much about animals – but Dick didn't *know* and he never would. He never would since she'd never let him. He had given her what she most wanted: she loved him still. She would die before she brought his head down.

97

12

The Security Executive as remodelled by the former Prime Minister had several advantages which in its older form it had not. The first was that the Prime Minister attended important meetings himself instead of having their outcome served up to him later when he would have to make a decision alone; and the second, just as important in practice, was the virtue of an elastic membership. A Board could coopt where a committee could not and today both Milden and Lord George had been called in. Both were deeply concerned with what had happened at Yeldham and it was essential to hear how they saw their positions. The other regular members were present, Charles Russell, the Commissioner of Metropolitan Police, the widely admired but tough-minded ex-Judge. The trendy bishop of Basingstoke was not. He hadn't in fact attended for months. This suited the other members well since he had only been put on the Board in the first place as a sop to the noisy Radical Chic.

Charles Russell thought the Prime Minister looked poorly. His skin had a sort of greyish pallor and his manner was less brisk than usual. But poorly or otherwise he was an excellent chairman. He was still quick and decisive and at moments abrasive and he had shown the point of the sword to Milden. Russell thought it had been skilfully done . . . Of course what had happened at the Milden establishment, what they'd agreed was a spy dropping out of the skies, was in no sense Mr Milden's fault, but that establishment was within a Minister's province and that Minister was Mr Milden. "Responsibility" had not been uttered but the implication had been both clear and hostile. Milden had simply nodded and said: "Quite so." Charles Russell had approved entirely. Milden knew the position but also the facts; he wasn't to be bogged down in excuses, in a self-justification he knew was unnecessary.

The Prime Minister had stared at him hard but had finally turned away to speak to Lord George. "Then the Foreign Secretary to speak," he said crisply. "What do you propose to do?"

Lord George answered him equally succinctly. "With your approval, Prime Minister, I propose to do nothing. The only evidence that man was American is that Maxe heard his voice and thought it so. Maxe didn't examine his clothes or his body but his weapon was certainly *not* American." Lord George permitted a frosty smile. "The people who arrange such things are very careful of detail indeed."

Charles Russell agreed; he had dealt with them often.

The Prime Minister asked: "But nothing whatever?"

"I would propose to convey an informal hint that we know very well who planned this outrage but I cannot do more for two very good reasons: the first is that we can't prove what we say and the second is that this isn't the moment to worsen relations already deteriorating."

"That course depends on a single man's silence. He isn't an official like his wife. He is bound by no rules."

"Dick Maxe?"

"Just so." The Prime Minister turned to the so far silent judge. By profession he was an excellent listener. "I believe you know Maxe."

"Quite well. I served with him. I know no man better at keeping his mouth shut."

"We'll have to accept the risk in any case."

"I do not think that risk a big one."

The Prime Minister shuffled the papers before him. It was a practised gesture and emitted a message: Foxy wanted the meeting over. But he still had another question to ask and he turned to Charles Russell to ask it shortly.

"So what happens now?" he enquired.

"I don't know."

"You would have made an excellent civil servant." It was reproof and was intended to be so.

Russell said blandly: "I very much doubt it."

Foxy started to say something more but checked it. Discourtesy to senior officials had been one of several varied reasons why his predecessor had fallen from power. He said politely enough but with the sting of acidity: "You're a man of wide and long experience. Give us its benefit, please. Make a guess."

Charles Russell had been hoping for this and was willing to talk on the basis of surmise. "I can't say there won't be other attempts but I would doubt if they will come at once. Along her tried and often successful lines Russia has had one failure already and if she sticks to the book as she normally does it will take her some time to mount another." He looked at Lord George in a silent enquiry and the Foreign Secretary nodded assent. "I understand that a certain Russian diplomat is to be withdrawn within a matter of days. In those days he can hardly do anything serious. He will know that his cover has gone, that he's suspect, and he'll assume that he's being shadowed day and night. That assumption will in fact be correct."

Foxy took a half minute off in thought. He wasn't fearful that in a matter of days Azimev could make fresh contacts at Yeldham but America was something else. Finally he swallowed and said:

"And America?"

"Your guess is as good as mine."

"What's yours?"

"If the big man can be made to think sensibly he'll tell the rough boys to lay off Yeldham. Instead he'll order his flocks of scientists to earn their keep, to get ANNE themselves and be quick about it. And with the enormous resources his country controls I wouldn't bet more than a pound that they won't."

"You really think that?"

"I think it's inevitable."

Lord George looked up at the ceiling and spoke to it. "In which case," he said, "we'd be empty handed. We shouldn't have a chip to bargain with."

Foxy was on the hook again; he would have liked to snub Lord George severely but he wasn't a man you could put down easily. Finally he found his formula. It was ponderous but it let him out.

"That's a matter for another place."

"*Peccavi*," Lord George said.

"Accepted." The Prime Minister had risen at last. "Then that concludes our business, I think. Good morning gentlemen and thank you." As they filed past him he added to Russell: "You'll continue to keep me in touch?"

"Of course."

Charles Russell took a cab to his club where he normally slept an hour after luncheon. He had a disciplined mind or his work would have killed him and on most days could summon sleep at will. But this morning he knew that he wouldn't succeed. He was unusually upset and edgy and a walk would do him more good than a restless nap. He put a roll in his pocket to feed the ducks and walked down to St. James's Park to do it.

He stood on the bridge and watched the pochard as Dick Maxe had watched the Canada geese. He hadn't enjoyed the tone of the morning's talk. The Prime Minister clearly detested Milden and Lord George's position had been faintly equivocal. He probably wouldn't bring Foxy down even if he had power to do so but if Foxy were slipping Lord George wouldn't catch him. Charles Russell shrugged in genuine indifference. The likes and dislikes of politicians, the ebb and flow of power in the Cabinet, were not in theory any part of his business but once they had involved him disastrously and he didn't wish to repeat the experience. With any luck that wouldn't recur but precedent could repeat itself cruelly.

He threw bread to a particularly handsome drake, aware he was breaking a rule and not caring. As for what was his official business, that two great powers wanted ANNE very badly, he'd told Foxy what he believed to be true. Russia might try again but not yet and America would concentrate on getting ANNE for herself as she surely would. When the enormous Soviet spying machine would be turned against another country. It looked like a rest between bouts of action but Charles Russell was too experienced to trust logic when an instinct spoke otherwise.

You had only to feel a moment's peace for some ghost to slip out of its cupboard and clobber you.

Arthur Milden had left the meeting with Lord George for he was buying him the lunch he owed him. In the taxi he told him: "I can't take you to a club. I don't have one. I'm not a very clubbable man."

"I wouldn't say that – it depends on the club. I know one which is full of professional chatterers, actors and lawyers and men from the media, and shattering bores they most of them are. And there's another where it isn't done to speak to another member at all unless you know him or have been introduced formally."

"That would suit me very well."

"Why not join, then? I could arrange it."

"Thank you, but I'm too much of a loner. Anyway, I like eating in restaurants. I'm taking you to one now." He named it.

Lord George said: "Splendid. Honest Italian food without chi-chi. I love it."

"I know you do."

"How do you know?"

"I ventured to ring Lady George."

"That was thoughtful. And what did she say?"

"She said you were a pig for pasta."

"She was perfectly right." Lord George considered. "To save you asking at table," he said, "I'll have an enormous plate of spaghetti to start with. None of that nonsense with mussels or cockles but plain *bolognese* with lots of sauce. After that I could manage an *ossobuco* and perhaps a little *dolcelatte* afterwards."

"I couldn't keep up with that."

"Don't try. And Italian wine is quite straightforward. There's some perfectly horrible wine in Italy though it isn't any worse than bad French but there's also some excellent stuff when you know it. It isn't a country for earnest wine snobs – no fuss about shippers or the wrong side of the hill. Order a reputable Barbera and you won't go far wrong. Avoid what they label Chianti at all costs. In fact the Chianti vineyards are tiny but if everything sold as Chianti in England were poured into a smallish pond you could float the Italian fleet on it comfortably."

They had two drinks in the bar and then went in. Milden

ordered as Lord George had asked, less enormously for his own consumption. "You know a lot about Italian food."

"I learnt it on the spot, in Italy. Would you care to hear the story?"

"Very much."

"Well, I wasn't dragged up in the orthodox manner, or not what people assume is orthodox for the sort of man I ostensibly am. I was sent to a public school all right, and after that the standard form is short service in the Brigade of Guards and then something in a merchant bank. But I didn't fancy a merchant bank and short service in the Brigade of Guards would have bored me beyond my limited tolerance. So I asked to continue my studies in Italy." Lord George belched lightly and then laughed happily. "I can assure you they were extremely catholic. But my father didn't like it a bit. He gave me a pretty mean allowance and younger sons don't get much when the great man dies. So I did the sensible thing and married an heiress. Mercifully we get on like a house on fire. Doubly lucky, you are thinking? You are right."

Arthur Milden was in fact thinking differently, wondering why this unusual grandee should be telling him what seemed purely private. He was to learn in time but not immediately for Lord George was off again in full cry.

"I'm talking about myself and boring you."

"Certainly not."

"Then I'll risk some more. I'm really an enormous fraud. We like it assumed that our founding father, the one who came over with Good King Billy, was some sort of courtier who had his ear. In fact he was the good king's barber. In those days that rather modest post included the tending of gentlemen's wigs and my distant ancestor was good at his job. He set up on his own and flourished exceedingly; he bought land with his savings, always land, and he imported a bride from darkest Holland. I have a reputation for a certain Dutch bluntness but it doesn't descend from an upper class gene."

"All that was a long time ago."

"It was. By Georgian times we were landed gentry but

we hadn't lost our nose for profit. German-speaking wee bit lairdies could sit on the throne and we didn't care. Provided they left the great Whig families to run the country and quietly enrich themselves. We were moving up the ladder now, ennobled and more titles to come. We were very big noises indeed, not like Foxy."

"Foxy?"

Lord George took a generous swig of Barbera. "Foxy is the typical Tory. He adores the Crown and the Church of England when in secret we don't give a fig for either. Foxy's ancestors were petty squires but they happened to have their land in Surrey where there's now a flourishing dormitory town. Foxy is far richer than I am but he suffers from something which I do not. Foxy is afraid like all of them. Fear is the glue of the Tory party, fear of losing what they've put together, the rich upper class Tories like Foxy himself down the line to the artisan doing well. I don't think that it can last much longer."

" 'It' being Foxy or just the system?"

"I don't approve of words like system and Foxy is safe for a little longer."

"I agree with what Russell was saying this morning. If the Americans get ANNE without us –"

"Very few people know ANNE exists and even fewer that we're bargaining bitterly. And outside my office and those concerned in the Cabinet almost nobody knows we're over-playing our hand. The Knights of the Shires in the House don't know, nor the prosperous bourgeoisie which keeps Foxy in power. When the Americans get ANNE, as they will, almost no one will know that he's made a balls."

"I once served in a Cabinet where you did not. I acquired quite a nose for the smell of unease."

"Which you are smelling again? I quite agree. But I don't think it's more than mid-term jitters."

"Suppose Foxy did go."

"I am not prepared to. In any case I should not be affected. I like being Foreign Secretary which suits my small talent for low Dutch cunning and I've no ambition to lead a party which at bottom I rather dislike and despise. By inherited instinct I'm an old-fashioned Whig. Prime Ministers nowadays work far too hard and as I told you I'm a family man."

Lord George was now on the *dolcelatte* and Milden watched him with a certain envy. When he'd finished it he said: "Thank you. The best meal I've had for several weeks. Now I'm ready to sing for my supper. Please listen."

"You've handsomely entertained me already."

"And you've been wondering why I've been talking as I have?"

"The thought had occurred."

"I will now resolve it. I am about to give you a serious warning and I wanted you to know where it came from. I didn't want you to think I was just another old school tie."

"If I'd ever thought that I shouldn't now."

"Then here it comes. Watch Foxy. He hates you."

"You told me that once before."

"I did. And you didn't pay the least attention. You went on saying that piece of yours about doing so many things better in Russia. I happen to agree but that's not the point. Then you made that silly speech in Cabinet about setting up a special police force. Again I agree and again it's irrelevant. I tried to warn you but you went on like a tank and got snubbed. Like an honest old tank and I rather admired you. But decency doesn't pay in politics. Foxy could have sacked you next morning."

"Why didn't he, then?"

"Because he didn't dare. He kept you on when your own lot fell because you had letters after your name in clusters and he thought you'd be a GP scientist who could advise on matters of science generally. When he found that you weren't that sort of scientist he felt a fool. But as I said before, he didn't dare drop you."

"I still can't think why."

"Because the previous Prime Minister was too good a butcher. In politics that is sometimes tolerated but not if the butcher too obviously enjoys it. Foxy couldn't risk a repetition of that especially when, as is happening now, there's a faint whiff of teacher's pets again."

"I've been lucky," Arthur Milden said.

"And you were luckier over that woman's mugging. I

realise it was really nothing but you happen to be a junior Minister and for several days the ruder Press ran it hard. Foxy didn't enjoy your publicity. He's shrewd and experienced but at bottom he's a second-rate hack. And all hacks like to hog the limelight alone. But there again he didn't dare sack you. You can't sack a man for preventing a mugging especially when it's on several front pages. So now I am formally, solemnly warning you. Don't give him another chance if you want to stay."

"I won't."

"Are you sure you're not doing just that? This telly thing of yours –" Lord George left it.

"You hear things," Milden said.

"I heard this one from Foxy himself as it happens. It's to be called *The Great at Play* or something equally catchpenny – scenes of important people playing their game. Foxy is playing cricket. Cricket!" Lord George waved a hand in dismissal, contemptuously. "Foxy hasn't a clue about cricket. I believe he got his house colours but that was all. He was all right against a straight up-and-downer, playing him off the front foot by the book, but to anything like a good off-spinner which at that time was something I happened to be he was the easiest of meat imaginable. He wasn't nippy enough to smother the spin and he hadn't been taught to sweep to leg. At that time that was considered inelegant, not a public school stroke at all, you know. But whatever you do you mustn't outshine him."

"I certainly won't at cricket. Literally that's not my scene."

"I gather it's some sort of wrestling."

"Well, not quite. It's something they call unarmed combat which I'm going to demonstrate with a respectable ex-Corporal of Horse."

"I still feel you should reconsider."

"I said I'd do it."

"There you go again – honest and decent. I told you before it didn't pay." Lord George stirred his coffee reflectively and said: "This is difficult to put convincingly but what's between you and boss-man Foxy is a long way from being purely political. The chemistry of love and hate is something we simply don't understand. Between people of different sexes it's simple: either the infection passes or it does not. But between man and man or woman and woman it's as mysterious as a theological doctrine. I only know that the thing exists. Foxy would like to do more than sack you; he would like to see you dead at his feet."

"As bad a sickness as that?"

"I suspect so." A calculated pause. "Or another."

"Another?"

"Rumours, of course – the barest whisper. But there's a platitude about smoke and fire."

Milden was woken at a quarter to twelve by a call from the police in south west London. The caller was a Superintendent. He was respectful but he was also firm. Mr Milden's daughter had been picked up soliciting.

Where was she now?

In the cells.

But surely –

Unhappily that wasn't all. In her bag had been a prohibited substance and the rules about that could not be bent.

Even, he'd thought, if he'd wished to bend them. He'd seen many Peggy Mildens and loathed them.

"I'll be down in the morning to arrange about bail."

"Very good, sir. Then I'll wish you good night."

They did some things very much better in Russia.

13

The media man who had thought it up had been complimented on a good idea and most of *The Great at Play* had already been shot. There'd been that eminent cleric who still played squash rackets, and that had emerged as bland as the man himself. The pro he'd been playing with had been feeding him cunningly but for his age he had some remarkable shots and once had honestly beaten the pro with a nick.

The producer had been pleased with that one and more with the next which had a certain wild beauty. The antibloodsports people would write in protesting but though they made a great deal of noise they weren't as numerous as they pretended to be and in any case weren't an organised lobby. So a Home Secretary had been shown shooting a pheasant. He was one of the top dozen shots in the country and he had done it with an enormous elegance. The mark had been high and flying fast but the Home Secretary had timed it perfectly. He had waited till it was almost vertical, swinging his weapon with it confidently, then fired a single shot from the choke. He hadn't looked round for he hadn't needed to. The bird had crumpled up in a ball, then fallen behind him in a diminishing parabola. It had looked as easy as eating corn.

The next episode had been Foxy himself in the plush little village the Prime Minister played for. As Lord George had said he could play up-and-downers and the opening bowlers had been brisk but innocuous. Foxy had put his left leg forward, driving at the pitch of the ball and making eighteen handsome runs, a highly presentable score in such cricket. But then the openers had been taken off and of the new men one was a classic off-spinner. He had once played minor counties cricket and though ageing still knew his business perfectly. He gave Foxy two standard break-backs, well pitched up, and Foxy got far enough forward to stun them. These balls had been well flighted and slow but the next was a good deal quicker and flatter. Foxy was obliged to play at it so he played back and got an inside edge. The wicketkeeper snapped it up gratefully.

Foxy had walked in in a very poor temper for he'd felt he was getting set for a fifty.

All these scenes had had to be shot outside but the final, which was Arthur Milden's, would be taken in the studio and tacked on live to the other three. Milden, mindful of Lord George's warning, had tried to back out but had found that he couldn't. The ex-Corporal of Horse was receiving a fee to say nothing of the free publicity and the producer had known where to hit Milden hardest. This, he had said, was a let-down. Mr Milden had promised.

So Arthur Milden had gone to the studio punctually where everything went disastrously wrong.

The first setback was a telephone call from the ex-Corporal of Horse who had been stricken with influenza suddenly. He had a temperature of a hundred and four and his wife was keeping him firmly in bed. In any case he was in no sort of shape convincingly to display his craft. Arthur Milden had snatched at this news as a let-out but the producer had overridden him sharply. Milden, he'd said again, had given his word and the fact that his partner was sick was irrelevant. He, the producer, would find another. All-in wrestlers were two a penny and although that pastime was no doubt different from the discipline which Milden would demonstrate, wrestlers knew how to roll and breakfall and most of them were pretty good actors, especially in the matter of feigning distress. The producer knew just the man for the job – he was fortunately on the staff of the studio. He picked up a telephone and talked fast and persuasively. Milden heard him mention the sum of three hundred pounds.

Arthur Milden walked on camera doubtfully. The little piece had been carefully rehearsed and fell into two disparate parts. In the first Milden would be the honest citizen walking home with a briefcase to tempt a mugger and the ex-Corporal Instructor would play that mugger. Milden would throw him but he'd get up and attack again. This time Milden would react more severely, apparently leaving the mugger insensible. The second part would be much more hairy, the roles reversed and the Instructor defending. Milden would charge with a naked bayonet and the Instructor would contemptuously disarm him.

It had been mutually agreed that this last part must go. Bayonets were not yet permitted in wrestling.

The red light went on and the compère began his spiel. He did it with grace and a certain tact, making no mention of any previous incident and introducing Arthur Milden as "Mr Milden" *tout court*. The camera swung to the left as the wrestler came in. "And now," the compère said with some relish, "we have the middleweight Gentleman Jim of Brixton who has kindly agreed to substitute for Mr Milden's original partner who has 'flu."

Arthur Milden froze in horror. Gentleman Jim was as black as coal.

There hadn't been time for a practice run-through for the outside scenes were already on the air. But Milden had been reassured that the wrestler understood his instructions: he was to attack Milden twice and be thrown about heavily. He had nodded. It was a piece of cake. Like all his trade he knew how to ham it. He could fall with a resounding crash without losing a breath or a single heartbeat. Milden had been reassured but he hadn't been told that the man was black.

He was in the cruellest dilemma and realised it instantly. To cast a convenient black as a mugger was something which telly must answer for later, the action of a desperate producer who would do anything to save his programme, but if he, Arthur Milden, walked away the watching millions would think only one thing. Arthur Milden was a rampant racist and no Minister could afford to risk that.

He sighed but he beckoned to Gentleman Jim.

Gentleman Jim had absorbed his instructions. He made a clumsy rush at Arthur Milden, trying to snatch that tempting briefcase. Milden dropped it, caught a hand and swung the arm. It was the whip again but not laid on hard and in any case Gentleman Jim knew the answer. He somersaulted neatly out of it and Milden knelt down and put on a leg-lock. Again he didn't put it on painfully but Gentleman Jim was furiously angry.

For he hadn't earned his nickname for nothing, priding himself that he always wrestled clean. He was known for this, half respected, half laughed at, but he stuck to it since it earned him bouts which he couldn't have otherwise hoped to obtain. And his opponent had fouled in the first few seconds; he had released his hold as the Gentleman rolled but immediately followed him down to the mat. He couldn't do that, it was grossly illegal. It was a basic rule and entirely necessary since without it the sport, if you called it that, would have further degenerated into a series of boring scrambles on the floor.

Gentleman Jim was a good clean wrestler and had listened to his instructions carefully but he'd assumed that the basic rules would be kept.

The leg-lock wasn't hurting him but he emitted the obligatory grunt. Then he broke the lock contemptuously and, still lying, put a leg-mare round Milden's neck. If he twisted and Milden didn't spin Milden would need an osteopath quickly.

But he didn't twist, he lay still and thought. He thought slowly but he wasn't stupid. This wasn't what he was being paid to do. He released the hold and both men stood up. Gentleman Jim had still to make the second attack.

He did so as he'd been told, fists flailing, and again Arthur Milden threw him heavily. He fell with a spectacular crash, not hurting himself in the least in doing so, but Milden had followed him down a second time. He was supposed to be unconscious but was not. He was up on his feet in a flash and waiting, and when Milden rose too he went at him seriously. He was as angry as he'd ever been. There was a tiny fleck of foam on his black lips.

Milden recognised authentic danger and he stopped Gentleman Jim in his tracks as he came in. He stopped him in the oldest way known to man. Gentleman Jim went down in a heap, holding his crutch. This time his cries of pain were real.

Somebody called "Cut" and they cut. But too late. The

programme was live and the fatal words uttered. Between his moans Gentleman Jim was articulate.

"Bloody Whitey."

Lord George very seldom watched television, preferring to chat to his wife or read, but this evening he had decided to do so. He had approved of the Home Secretary's marksmanship, chuckled at the Prime Minister's downfall, but when he saw Milden and Gentleman Jim he groaned.

The Prime Minister was already in very low spirits for he considered that he'd been shabbily treated. The cricketing scene in his rich little village had shown nothing of his eighteen handsome runs, only his getting out like a duffer to a stroke which the rawest beginner was taught to eschew. They had shown his return to the pavilion he'd paid for, the scowl of disappointment on his face. There'd been some polite applause and this had come over. There *had* to be some polite applause: not every village could field a Prime Minister and this one had been a generous patron. Foxy thought that they'd wickedly underplayed him.

So he was in an ugly mood when Arthur Milden came up, disappointed and a little resentful, ready to flame into something more violent. He had heard the piece about somebody catching 'flu but knew nothing of a producer's decision to take the only man immediately available to save his programme from total collapse. What he saw was a white man fighting a black and dropping him with a flagrant foul. That white man was Arthur Milden, a Minister.

The unfairness struck him before the crime: he, Foxy, would have to dodge the brickbats, the House exchange would fuse up with protests. First there would be that woman from Hampstead, the high priestess of the disdainful Left. She already disapproved of wrestling, calling it an ignoble spectacle and urging Foxy to have it stopped along with boxing and of course all blood sports. A secretary could deal with her as she'd been dealt with more than once in the past but after her would come much heavier metal, the strident voices of those who smelt racism in every unlikely event of the day. And in this one a black man had been humiliated publicly, his audible comment had been entirely justified. Foxy couldn't avoid a solemn question in the House.

And that was where the crime came in for the Prime Minister didn't desire such a question. Lord George had spoken of mid-term jitters but Foxy had sensed there was more than that. If the long knives weren't out and presently after him they were being increasingly whetted behind his back. And here was a junior Minister doing something to give them a sharper edge.

Foxy's furious anger cooled to frustration for there was nothing in the world he could do. Milden couldn't be sacked – Foxy dare not do so. A year ago he might well have dismissed him but a year ago he'd been thought to be useful and the circumstances were different now. The Prime Minister was experienced and could smell the increasing malaise around him. Traditional Tory paternalism had not been enough; it had in fact set the country back sharply. A palace revolution had brought him to power: another could as easily break him. One reason for his predecessor's fall had been that she'd wielded the cleaver far too lustily and in any case the High Tory tradition was to stick to your colleagues through thick and thin, through anything short of some sexual scandal which, it was agreed but not said, was the sin against the Holy Ghost, since it lost more votes in the faithful suburbs than did bitter unemployment in the north.

He had schemed for the previous Prime Minister's fall but in one thing he had entirely agreed with her, a hatred of the fetid sham which called itself better race relations, the knighted front men of what was called the New Commonwealth. Which of these statelings would lift a finger if Britain were attacked or fell on hard times? A rhetorical question, Foxy decided. Meanwhile they held their begging bowls out with all the arrogance of a Buddhist monk, proud of their uncontrolled incontinence, demanding aid as a matter of right from countries which they privately hated.

The Prime Minister sighed. He'd throw an enemy to the lions with pleasure but not a colleague to these mangy jackals. He'd have to defend a man he hated. Damn him, damn him, damn him, damn him.

The Prime Minister, like Lord George, groaned audibly but not for the identical reason. The pain had started up again and each bout was a little worse than the last.

14

When they'd motored back from Yeldham together Charles Russell had asked Milden to lunch at his club. Events had prevented the meeting maturing but Russell was a punctilious man who liked to keep a given engagement and the invitation had been renewed and accepted. Now the porter was announcing his guest's arrival and Russell was helping him out of his coat in the hall. "Delighted you could come," he said. "The bar's pretty pokey and is sure to be crowded. Let's be comfortable in the smoking room."

They sat down in the splendidly shabby old room and ordered drinks. Arthur Milden was looking round unashamedly, at the elegant Chinese-Chippendale mirror, the full length portraits of grandees in uniform. Most were of respectable vintage but one was a good deal newer, a woman. She was bare-shouldered in a long black gown and wore a good deal of faintly flashy jewellery. Charles Russell saw Milden's inspection return to her.

"A duke's mistress," he said. "I've forgotten which. The man left it to the club when he died. As his legitimate grandson is still a member we can hardly take it down."

"You should." It had sounded emphatic.

"There's a school of thought which certainly thinks so."

"If I were a member I'd promptly join it. Do you mind if I have a closer look?"

They got up and stood in front of the portrait. Charles Russell knew very little of painting – in the world of the arts he loved Persian rugs – but his instinct was that this portrait was somehow wrong. Enormously skilled but entirely hollow.

Arthur Milden said: "A Gabor, I see. A Hungarian mountebank. Made a fortune in the 'twenties with this stuff."

Russell peered at the plaque. He had seen it a thousand

times and never noticed the name. "The Honourable Mrs Godspeed," he said. "By Lajos Gabor."

"I hate it. It offends me."

"I've a glimmering of what you mean."

"I apologise – I've been very rude. But there's a story about Lajos Gabor. Someone once asked an eminent critic what was the best way to look at his portraits. The answer was in a coal mine at midnight."

They went back to their sofa to finish their drinks and Charles Russell to some quiet thinking. From the little he had seen of Milden he had liked him and in a real sense respected him. He'd been successful in a competitive business and successful in his politics too till the Old Gang had rebelled and removed the New. Outside the political free-for-all too Arthur Milden seemed to have few private friends and none of the supportive background of even an averagely successful marriage. He was suspect of a streak of machismo and a woman would be the first to resent it.

And here was this successful insensitive showing shocked and clearly genuine emotion over a meretricious portrait which gave him offence. This man was much more complex than he appeared.

They went up to the dining room, ordering their meal, and Russell noticed that Milden ate heartily. He said with an understanding smile:

"Catching up on the hospital food? That's sensible."

"No, not exactly. The hospital food was wholesome and ample but it *was* a little dull and starchy."

"I noticed you refused a roll."

"That's the trouble, you see. I've put on more weight than I'll easily lose. But in other ways the hospital was admirable. They kept out the Press till I was ready to talk to them."

"I saw some of the headlines," Charles Russell said. "What's it like to be a three-day hero?"

"Personally I notice no difference but I dare say it has improved my image." Milden looked at Charles Russell, weighing him carefully; finally he said deliberately: "It is difficult to dismiss a hero."

"But the man with power to dismiss may resent him."

This time Milden's glance was sharp. "You see it like that?"

"I'm afraid I do."

"To be honest with you so do I. For a month or two I'm probably safer but after that I'm more vulnerable than ever."

"You're a realist."

"I have to be."

Milden had had two gin and tonics and maybe half a carafe of wine. He was a long way from drunk but he didn't drink regularly and the wine had pleasantly loosened his tongue. "And in two ways I was bloody lucky in an action which was entirely reflex. I put out that mugger's shoulder. Violence! But the man had a knife and he certainly used it. There'll be no nonsense about excessive force."

"You've been reassured on that?"

"More or less."

"Then what was the second piece of luck?"

"The man was white."

Charles Russell very slightly stiffened. He hadn't been watching telly the night before and his newspaper, a staid old blatt, hadn't thought the incident worth a mention. He wasn't to know that others were screaming it. What he feared was a lecture on Race Relations. His private opinion was firm and unshaken: immigration had been an unshriven crime, the bill still to pay by the next generation. But by that time, with any luck, he'd be dead. So there it was and now they must live with it. It wasn't a subject for luncheon at a club.

He changed the conversation smoothly. "Let's have some coffee downstairs."

"I'd like to."

They settled again in the emptying smoking room and Charles Russell began on a different subject. He had met Milden twice and read his file, and of the two the meetings had told him the more. Milden's file had been that of hundreds of others. A record of a successful man's progress, little more than could be got from *Who's Who*. But it recorded that Milden had worked in Russia. Russell had been curious, had asked for a further report and got it. It had recorded the facts: now he wanted the comment. Men who'd responsibly worked in Russia weren't as common as daisies on summer lawns.

"I'm told that you once worked in Russia."

Arthur Milden had declined a brandy but he was still talking easily and continued to do so. "I did. And not as a diplomat or a visiting fireman. I had an ordinary commercial job for my firm. I led a normal life with normal Russians."

"Care to give me the picture? You know what I do and it's mostly political. An insight into day-to-day life, day-to-day work and day-to-day Russians is something very hard to come by."

"I won't be boring you?"

"Certainly not."

"Then it was my first big job but it wasn't in Russia. Or rather not in Russia proper – it was deep in the heart of Kazakhstan. The town called itself a provincial capital and they were developing land round it for cotton. For that they needed a great deal of water and for the water they needed a great deal of power. That was where I came in. Electricity."

"Did you enjoy it?"

"At first I loathed it. Their system is appallingly central-ised and to begin with they were stiff and suspicious. But once they'd made up their minds that I wasn't a spy, once they'd decided that I knew my job, they'd do anything you asked on your nod. We finished that job well ahead of schedule. Think of that happening here and weep. The Unions would make it impossible."

Russell let that one go by discreetly. "And the personal aspect?" he asked.

"Not at all bad. The real Russians have colonised Kazakh-stan but there are still Kazakhs left and I liked them enor-mously. One of them got me out of a scrape."

"May I ask what sort?"

"A woman, of course. I don't really like women but I can't live without one. The usual thing."

"You mean she turned out to be some sort of agent?"

"No, I don't think so."

"It's the classic ploy."

"She was much too stupid to be anyone's agent."

"There are women who'd have your balls for that."

"But they're not the sort of women I fancy."

. . . No wonder this man's affairs break up quickly.

"Then what was this scrape?"

"The other usual thing with a woman. She complained that I had seduced her. I had not. She complained that she was in pup. She was not. Her parents started to make a fuss. Very serious for a foreigner."

"Very. And your friend had sufficient influence to pull you out of that one?"

"He had. He was a Kazakh but his name had been heavily Russianised. He was bright and was climbing the ladder fast. He's in London, as it happens, now."

"Have you been seeing him?"

"No. I didn't dare. He wrote to me a year ago and I had him checked. I didn't need to go as high as you."

"And what were you told?"

"To ignore the letter."

Charles Russell frowned. The advice had been perfectly sound and orthodox but wholly without imagination, the advice of some played-out old hack past promotion. He himself would have given the same but wrapped it up. No contact with this man whatever, but a polite little note explaining why. Milden was now a Minister and had to be careful in social contacts. Words to that effect but put better. As it was Milden would have made an enemy and a Russian who was also a Kazakh wasn't something to be tangled with lightly.

An alarm bell rang suddenly, loud and insistent. Charles Russell didn't believe in accident, it was a word for the detached intellectual reluctant to face the real world around him. Where everything finally formed a pattern. The old gods played dice to pass an evening and if they threw two sixes two sixes you got . . . A Kazakh who had been working in London, a Kazakh who had been spying at Yeldham, a Kazakh who had written to Milden and been snubbed . . .

He had thought of a ghost creeping out and clobbering him and this one held an outsize cosh.

Russell's brain was racing but his manner still cool. Finesse was now pointless; he asked directly: "You said your friend worked in London. Where?"

119

"At the Russian Trade Mission. When I asked about him they said that made it worse."

"It did. And it's worse if the man's name was Azimev."

Milden was astonished, showed it. "How did you know that?"

"Because Azimev has been caught out spying. He is being expelled tomorrow at ten o'clock."

Milden had gone white but said levelly: "That's something, I suppose. Only nineteen hours –"

"I wouldn't be too sure of it – try to see it from Azimev's point of view. He has a guaranteed seat on an aircraft tomorrow. If you were he, planning further mischief, you'd leave action to the last possible moment."

"I hadn't thought of that."

"You should."

"But what possible mischief?"

"I do not know. There was a time when I had to think Russian and did so but I can't pretend to think like a Kazakh. All I know is that you have made an enemy."

"You take that seriously?"

Russell nodded.

Milden said soberly: "So do I. An affront is still an insult to be avenged."

"Then what are you doing this evening?"

"I'm staying in."

"Good. Expecting any visitors?"

"My daughter." He was tempted to add "who's in serious trouble", but this wasn't the moment for tea and sympathy.

"You live in a flat, I believe."

"I do."

"Can you release the front door from inside it?"

"No, I'm afraid you can't. It's old-fashioned."

"So you have to go down to the front door yourself? Be careful when you do so."

"Oh, I will."

"Admit your daughter but nobody else. I'll put a man on your block to do what he can."

"Thank you very much." Milden rose. "And thank you for luncheon."

"I'm sorry it was spoilt like this."

120

Russell saw Milden out politely. A taxi was setting down and Milden took it. Russell noticed that he was entirely steady. The Arthur Mildens were hard to scare.

Russell went back into the club and rang Lord George. There was a good deal of tedious explanation but finally he got through to him personally. "Charles Russell here. We've met at the Executive."

"I remember very well." It was friendly.

"I understand that a certain official is due to leave the country tomorrow."

"That is correct. On the ten o'clock Aeroflot." Lord George had caught the note of urgency. "Has anything gone wrong?"

"Not yet but it very easily could."

"Something I ought to know?"

"Most certainly. I'll tell you later but not on this line."

"I understand. But if we're thinking of the same official you'll remember that *non grata* or otherwise he still has a quasi-diplomat's status."

"I wasn't thinking of arresting him."

"Good. And if you're thinking of anything else make it credible."

"Unhappily I'm on the defensive."

"I'm sorry to hear that. Till we meet."

15

When he'd finished his chat to Lord George at the Foreign Office Charles Russell drove straight to the Security Executive. There he summoned his most senior operator and repeated what Arthur Milden had told him.

The operator said briefly: "Messy."

"Very messy indeed, so let's eliminate. I don't think there can be any question of blackmail. The fact that Azimev did Milden a favour does not in itself expose Milden to pressure but is an excellent reason why Azimev would expect that Milden would return the kindness when he could."

"Which he didn't; he brushed Azimev off. A very dangerous thing to do with the sort of man who values face highly."

"Exactly what I'm afraid of myself but I think we can also eliminate violence. We're agreed that Azimev's taken this badly but there's no evidence he is also mad. Anything in the nature of violence, something outside his own sacrosanct embassy, and the Geneva Convention might well not protect him. That would be a matter for lawyers and could easily drag on for months, but the Russians don't care for junior officials who overstep their instructions badly and land them in international embarrassment. They might decide to waive his formal status and present themselves as the good neighbours they are not. Azimev would know all that and Azimev is no man's fool. I'm convinced he would think the risk too high."

"There are other kinds of mayhem than physical."

"Again what I was thinking. Such as what?"

"Some smear which Milden couldn't wash out. Something sufficiently, inescapably compromising to finish his career in politics."

Charles Russell nodded. "Yes, we're thinking the same. But how could Azimev fix it?"

"I don't know."

"Then we're back on the blind defensive which I detest. I take it Azimev is under surveillance?"

"Routine surveillance – nothing more has been necessary. He has gone nowhere except to his office and home again."

"So if he went to Milden's flat he'd be shadowed?"

"Certainly he'd be shadowed, sir. But I take it he shouldn't be stopped, short of violence."

"Correct and we've discounted that. But put a man on Milden's house just in case."

"I'll go myself."

"That's excellent news if nothing else is."

Russell started to rise but the operator stopped him. "One small point of detail, please. You said that his daughter is calling this evening and that he has to go down to let her in?"

"That's what he said."

"His daughter is in serious trouble."

"Better tell me," Russell said. He sat down again.

"She's a drop-out who has gone downhill fast. She works, or rather she did till they sacked her, for a suspect African organisation. She's had lovers of every shape and colour. Her father gives her a fair allowance but apparently it isn't enough. Last night the police picked her up for soliciting."

"Bad," Russell said.

"And worse to come. In her bag was what our friends the police so delicately call a prohibited substance."

"Cannabis?"

"No, she's worked through that. It was the hard stuff. Heroin. She's now on bail."

"If I were religious I'd pray for Milden."

"I am and I have. But that isn't the point."

"What is it, then?"

"A hunch. A premonition. Nothing."

"Out with it, man."

"It's simply that the thought had occurred that an addict will do anything for a supply of the drug on which she's hooked. And this one is visiting Milden this evening."

★

Azimev's recall had shattered him for he knew what it meant to his future prospects. To have failed was one thing, serious enough, but to have been blown and formally recalled was another, a very big black mark indeed. If he'd ever had any doubt of that his new posting would have removed it harshly. He was to report back to Moscow where they wouldn't speak softly and thereafter was to proceed to Dacca.

Bangladesh, he thought. The Almighty, if there were such a thing, had had a very off day when he'd created Bangladesh. An appalling climate, floods and famines, a philoprogenitive people which bred like fleas. Even Indians despised them heartily. Azimev was an ambitious man and this was many steps down promotion's ladder.

He was bitter as he thought of Milden. He had never intended to try to blackmail him since he hadn't the smallest lever to do so. When Azimev had written to him he'd been behaving as he'd been told to behave, which was to keep a low profile and hands quite clean till the order came to do something more active. And Milden could have been more than helpful to a middle-rank quasi-diplomat making his way. Yeldham was under Milden's Ministry but Azimev hadn't supposed for a moment that he'd give him whatever was ANNE's strange secret, even if he knew what it was, which Azimev had been instructed to doubt.

No, but he could have done other things helpful, the introductions to men in another world, the entry into a different society, something outside the closed circuit of diplomats. The possession of these earned high marks with his seniors and one could never tell what they might not lead to when the order came through to change one's role.

And Milden hadn't answered his letter.

A sudden rage shook him, entirely personal. He had been snubbed like an importunate beggar. His name was now Azimev but his father's had not been. He had ancient blood in his veins, vaguely holy; he had been treated as an upstart and he was not. He wasn't thinking of ANNE by now but of a personal score which demanded settlement. Dacca would be bad enough but the sentence would be the harder to serve if the feudal generations behind him nagged incessantly that he'd ignored their rules.

124

Well, he could break Milden decisively. It would have been one thing for a plain official, newly arrived and unsuspected, to have called on a man he had known in Russia; it would be another and inescapably compromising if a known spy were to contact a junior Minister the evening before he was expelled from the country.

He had made his plan with a solid competence, using the single weapon he had which had come to him in his days of training. For agents who were posted to London weren't immediately pitched into serious spying. For three months they kept strictly within their cover, learning the language and what they could of the people, doing nothing outside their official credentials. Then there was something they called the kitchen. Azimev had detested the months he had spent in it for it was a life which he despised and loathed, the sleazy world of the Left-leaning drop-outs, the haters of all established order, rebels without a cause defined and in any case lacking the will to fight for it. It would have been pointless to try to recruit such people, undisciplined and quite unindoctrinated, but they possessed a single gift to an agent.

That gift was scandal for all scandal was mischief and all mischief a part of the global war. Most of the time what they gave was useless, the idle chatter of a decadent people, but just occasionally they could give you a lead, something for men higher up to work on. A key agent had quietly disappeared. An able soldier in NATO had had to leave it under a cloud.

In this degenerate and futile desert Azimev had met one man he respected. He was a black who had been chased out of South Africa and who now worked for the same front as Peggy Milden. He hated all whites and avenged himself cruelly; he sold them hard drugs and rejoiced at their misery; and he'd told Azimev that Peggy Milden was hooked.

Azimev had passed that on, though he hadn't expected much to come of it . . . The daughter of a junior Minister and in any case they could hush it up. It wasn't close enough to the quick to hurt and in fact had never been followed up by those whose business it was to decide to. In the global war it hadn't been big enough but in Azimev's private war against Milden it was a formidable weapon indeed.

He had discussed his plan with the black South African who had smiled wickedly and at once agreed. Yes, he could manage the first part quite easily; he could arrange that all supplies to Miss Milden be cut off till she'd obeyed her instructions.

What were those instructions?

Azimev told him.

"It's going to need careful timing but it's on."

The operator watching Milden's house saw several things happen at once and was puzzled. The first was Peggy Milden's arrival. He had expected that but not her escort. A black had been in the taxi with her but since he stayed in it the operator didn't move. Peggy went up the steps and rang the bell. Her father opened it and something went wrong. There was a light in the porch and the watcher saw clearly. There seemed to be some sort of argument. Milden had hold of his daughter's arm and was apparently trying to pull her inside. Peggy was resisting furiously, looking behind at the street, weeping miserably. They were both of them still in the doorway, framed in it.

A car came up from nowhere and stopped. Two men got out and one was Azimev. The other seemed to be holding a camera. Azimev ran up the steps and faced the street. He put himself between Milden and Peggy, linking his right arm with Milden's left, putting his left round Peggy's waist. He was smiling his most social smile.

A flashbulb popped and the scene dissolved. Peggy ran down the steps to the black man. Azimev returned to the car which drove away. Arthur Milden stood for a moment, frozen, then went back into the house alone.

The operator ran to the nearest telephone.

At the airport next morning Azimev noticed his shadow. He wasn't in the least put out by him since he guessed that he wasn't there to stop him but only to make sure that he left. He followed Azimev through Departure doggedly, then out in the bus to the waiting aircraft. When Azimev boarded he raised his hat.

126

Azimev settled for the long boring flight. He was going home to a reprimand and then to a penal station called Dacca. Where, he had decided, he'd die, of cholera or dysentery or clap. Or maybe simply rot with boredom.

That wouldn't matter since when he went he'd be well received on the other side. His ancestors would understand. In a degenerate society where a man couldn't go armed against an enemy the full rigour of the rules must be relaxed. But allowing for that he hadn't shamed them.

16

The Prime Minister's mail was carefully screened for there had been letter bombs, mostly amateurish, and once or twice parcels which, though less dangerous, were considerably more offensive. So the quarto envelope had been through the scanner and the junior secretary opened it confidently.

She pulled out the photograph and looked at it, puzzled. Two men and a girl stood on a doorstep. She recognised one man as Milden but the other with his arm in the Minister's, smiling that "I'm at home here" smile, was somebody she didn't know. The woman appeared to be weeping miserably. There was no sort of caption to go with the photograph.

Curious.

The man beside her was slightly her senior and she passed him the photograph, raising her eyebrows. He was puzzled in turn but came back in half an hour looking shaken with a slip of paper bearing three names which he clipped to the photograph. "Send that on to the senior staff and pray for them."

When the photograph finally reached the Prime Minister his first feeling was one of satisfaction: he had Milden where he wanted him at last. He took a dose of the drug which the doctor had given him and as the pain eased momentarily his mind cleared with it. So did his all too brief euphoria. For this photograph made a private vendetta look foolish. That had been a nagging frustration but this thing on his desk did much more than nag; it tore at his agonised bowels when the pain did not.

It was true that he could now dismiss Milden but the price of that would be far too high. Give a reason for dismissing him, that he'd been the contact of a Russian spy, and immediately there'd be a resounding scandal. It might be big enough to bring down his government and he intended to stay in power while he could. Or sack him in mid-term without reason and the press would smell a body and dig it out. Every journalist worth the name would start ferreting and one of them would get to the truth in time. When the result would be the same, a scandal . . . An innocent relationship from a friendship in another life? Very possibly true but who would believe it? It was difficult to prove a negative. Suspicion would always be there and would stick. The Opposition would make an enormous meal of it.

He summoned a middle-rank secretary and told him: "Get Colonel Charles Russell round here immediately. Wherever he may be. Take a car and this photograph. Show it to Russell."

He dispatched his more important business and settled to think of a private problem. For he had some time to tell his wife he was dying and he feared doing that rather more than the fact.

She was a determined woman who had done some simple nursing in the war and, like many who had worked in a hospital, had unshakeable opinions and theories on every medical subject known to man. Foxy had asked for it straight and been given it: exploratory surgery could be undertaken if he insisted on it but the chances of its proving successful were not, in this honest surgeon's view, sufficient to make it a sensible option. Foxy who wasn't a coward had taken that but he didn't want it stirred up in domestic strife. Which his wife would assuredly do and keep on at it. She would insist on what she'd call second opinions when he knew that he'd had the best available; she'd talk about those places in Switzerland which were known to have succeeded dramatically.

. . . Which *claimed* to have succeeded dramatically. Doctors didn't seem to think so.

Doctors talked their own book. They had to. Anyone who had worked in a hospital knew how they covered up like lawyers.

The Prime Minister shuddered, he couldn't face it. One day he'd have to but not this morning. Not with this business of Arthur Milden still in the air and undecided. Charles Russell could help in that. He must.

Foxy received him politely and offered a drink. Russell declined with an equal courtesy. He had attended with a quiet reluctance since he had taken his own decision easily. Arthur Milden was all sorts of problem politically but he wasn't any threat to security. Charles Russell was well paid to guard that but it wasn't any part of his business to pull political chestnuts from political fires.

He watched Foxy as he began to talk, thinking he looked extremely ill. He had heard rumours but had discounted them strongly. Foxy wasn't the type to go down easily. But now he was inclined to credit them. The Prime Minister was a very sick man and sick men could make outrageous demands. Moreover one must treat them gently, one couldn't just slap them down and walk away.

It was going to be a difficult interview.

Russell had passed back the photograph silently. "That's dynamite," Foxy said.

"I don't dissent."

"Then what do you propose to do?"

"Nothing. It is not my business."

"But Milden is a threat to security."

"With respect, Prime Minister, I do not think so. Whatever may be the secret of ANNE it isn't one which Milden knows."

"But he could get it."

"Possibly. As a matter of theory I have to concede it. What I do not concede is why he should."

"He has an established connection with Russia."

"True. One dating back to a job twelve years ago."

"Listen," the Prime Minister said. "A quasi-diplomat has been declared *non grata* and we now know he was also a spy. The last thing he does before leaving the country is to call on Arthur Milden openly. Tell me why he did that."

"I cannot. But I'm prepared to make a guess from experience, from some knowledge of the mind of spies. I would guess it was simple retaliation. He had been snubbed and was going home to a reprimand."

"I don't agree with that."

"I'm sorry."

A sudden spasm seized Foxy visibly, his face contorted,

he audibly gasped. He took something from a pocket and swallowed it. Russell watched him with a genuine sympathy. Like Foxy he didn't fear death, or not overly, but pain he feared beyond all else. The Prime Minister said with an admirable stoicism: "I apologise for that."

"Not at all."

. . . He's even sicker than it looks. Here it comes.

"I still think Arthur Milden's a danger."

"Politically? Yes, I quite see that."

"I am asking for your help."

"In what way?" Russell had guessed precisely in what way.

"It would be a convenience if Arthur Milden disappeared. There could still be a scandal but a very much smaller one. Scandals about the dead aren't front page news."

Charles Russell disapproved of euphemism but this wasn't the moment for a lecture on plain words. "I'm afraid I cannot help you in that."

"I don't see why not. You have done it before."

It was a grossly unfair blow and Russell blinked. Ordinarily he would have reacted angrily but he had seen what he had seen and been touched. He controlled a rising anger and said: "In the words of the schoolmen I'm obliged to distinguish. I have had men killed when they endangered the country. I was paid to do that and it didn't disturb me." He hesitated but finally said it: "Private assassinations I do not accept."

"Another man might," the Prime Minister said.

Russell looked at him, a little uncertain. He seemed to be out of pain for the moment but he was still seriously and visibly ill.

Charles Russell thought it over, then said: "I think you have it a little wrong. I've been dropped from the Executive before and survived. I have a pension and a little money, outside interests which I could easily increase. But if you're asking for my resignation I'll write it out now if you'll give me paper."

The Prime Minister said: "I'll consider that."

"And whilst you are doing so one other point. The Executive isn't a private army. I take the chair when you're not attending yourself but there are other Board-members with minds of their own. I don't include that foolish priest who was put where he is as a sort of cosmetic and who in any case hasn't attended for months but in the matter of purely political killing I know two others who would kick like mules."

The Prime Minister said with a hint of entreaty: "You're not being very helpful."

"I cannot."

"Then two small requests before you leave. You will say nothing of what we've discussed this morning?"

"That would be very improper indeed."

"And nothing of what you have seen of myself?"

"That has only my sincerest sympathy. Moreover I am not a gossip."

Charles Russell went back to his flat to think for he had another and much more serious worry. The embarrassments of Prime Ministers were not something which he was fee'd to relieve but security very surely was and the newspapers were making alarming reading. The Middle East was in turmoil again and on that Charles Russell's view was simple, that which had been his statesman great-uncle's when the Ottoman Empire had been falling to pieces. The situation was hopeless but never serious. The fact that one clan of Arabs was murdering another was something which Russell could bear with fortitude but if by some miracle so far ungranted they managed to cohere for once, turn on Israel as an effective alliance . . . He didn't himself think that likely to happen but he knew someone else who actively feared it.

Judith Maxe. Judith Maxe who held the key to ANNE.

She had talked to him with astonishing candour, admitting in the plain words he admired that if her people should find themselves backs-to-the-sea that would weigh with her more than her formal duty. Bravado? Charles Russell thought not. She was known to be a passionate Zionist and she clearly hadn't thought him a fool. She had taken it entirely for granted that the thought would have occurred already, as indeed it had and more than once. But only as a vague hypothesis: now, on what he read in his papers, it was a calculable chance which it was his business to calculate.

So if she took action what form would it take? Charles Russell shrugged; he had no idea. There was something very odd about ANNE, something frighteningly unscientific. Things happened at Yeldham which didn't elsewhere, the same process succeeding one day, failing the next. When he'd pointed out the established fact that when she, Judith Maxe, was in charge herself the average of success rose sharply she had teased him with chat of some feminine mystery. But was there a secret within a secret? In the world of science such things didn't happen.

He corrected himself. They hadn't so far.

Of one thing he was entirely convinced: she wouldn't demean herself by any act of a spy, smuggling out papers through drops or go-betweens. If she betrayed her trust she would do it personally. Judith Maxe would defect to Israel.

Russell nodded, more sure than ever. He had met her and admired her greatly. Her instinct in this matter would be his own. If his country were in serious trouble, foreign troops on its soil, its people starving, he would wish to be in England and armed. Judith would feel the same – and he knew it.

Except that Judith wouldn't be bearing arms; she'd be bearing something more valuable – ANNE.

He took a taxi to the Security Executive and there he gave simple orders crisply. Judith Maxe was to be discreetly watched. Very discreetly – the best men available. If she tried to leave the country she must be stopped but no other action of any kind should be taken without his express approval.

Dick Maxe had come down to Yeldham again though this wasn't a time in the farmer's year when a good one liked to leave his land. But Judith had been increasingly edgy, nervous and under some private stress, and Dick Maxe was a conscientious husband.

He was returning from the island this morning where he'd gone at first light to inspect the geese. The goslings were afloat and feeding and he waved to them in satisfaction. Canada geese were fickle fowl and gunfire could have disturbed the pair permanently. He didn't bother to look at the hide where an unknown man, presumed American, lay buried without benefit of priest. The thought in no way disturbed Dick Maxe. Such men were beyond his established pale.

He pulled the punt back to the mainland thoughtfully, walking across to the house and his breakfast. He knocked on his wife's bedroom door. She was doing her face but turned it to him. "Breakfast in twenty minutes?" he asked. He was wearing Wellingtons and a boiler suit. "That'll give me time to change these clothes."

"I'll make you a good one."

"I could certainly use it."

He changed and went down to the comfortable kitchen, moving with his deliberate but still springy stride. The breakfast, as promised, was good and ample and he ate it with the appetite of a man who had been up for a couple of hours. His wife, he noticed, ate almost nothing and of small talk she had nothing at all. Normally she amused him royally. She never talked shop for the very good reason that he wouldn't have understood a word but she was interested in politics generally and she gave him what life in the country could not.

There were rumours about the Prime Minister's health and darker rumours about discontent in the Cabinet. A private palace revolution had put Foxy where he was today: another could as easily break him. Hard-nosed Victorian *laissez faire* had been too much for the traditional Tories who had quietly replaced its priests and practitioners but the traditional Tories were making a nonsense and Judith wondered what would happen next. Probably back to consensus politics and the irreversible drift into mediocrity. It wasn't a pleasant prospect but there you were.

Dick Maxe had been missing such talk acutely not only because he had greatly enjoyed it but because he had guessed why his wife had withheld it. Judith Maxe was very near her limit.

He decided to offer his wife an opening. She might very well decline to take it but if she did it might offer a moment's relief. He was an experienced and considerate husband. He

had made his guess about what was troubling her and opened
the conversation by saying:

"There are newspapers in Norfolk too."

She seemed to accept that gladly and smiled. "I know
there are. Which ones do you read?"

"I read the *Telegraph* and the *Financial Times*. A farming
journal. That's the lot."

"The orthodox views?"

"You could properly say so."

"I see a good deal more than that."

"That I had guessed," he said. In fact he knew. He had
seen letters with Israeli stamps and some of them had looked
official.

He could see that she was tempted to talk but she hadn't
quite made up her mind to do so. Instead she threw the ball
back to her husband.

"What do you make of the Middle East?"

"The Middle East is mostly Arabs." He pronounced it
Ay-rabs in unconscious contempt. He had seen them in his
war and turned his head.

"There are an awful lot of them. And we can't take
casualties."

"Also they're the world's worst soldiers. Their idea of a
battle is a gun-duel with artillery. They do that with enormous gusto. But they don't aim at each other's batteries.
That would be dangerous. They just knock the other side's
towns into rubble. You say you can't take casualties. They
won't."

"Is that the accepted view in Norfolk?"

"I expect you'll find it goes further than Norfolk."

Judith Maxe said: "I do not share it."

She was relaxing now: he dared ask direct questions.
"Why not?" he said.

"It goes back to America."

"I don't follow that."

"It's alarmingly simple. America gives us a technical edge,
sufficient to balance inferior numbers. But she may not
always do that. *I am afraid.*"

"The Jewish lobby," he said. "The votes of American
Jews. There are a lot."

"The Jewish lobby is admittedly powerful. Also it is increasingly resented, particularly in the American heartland. I don't think it at all impossible that a President of the United States could be elected without its votes behind him."

He thought that over before he said: "Personally I think that improbable. But I have to admit it's on the cards."

"In which case bang goes our technical edge." She hesitated but finally said it. "*Unless there were somebody else to restore it.*"

He was quick and said: "Don't do it, love."

"I didn't say I was going to."

"True. In any case how *could* you do it? Your position is far too exposed for treason. Try to pass anything on and they'd get you."

She reacted as Russell had thought she would, turning the suggestion down contemptuously. "That's dirty and I wouldn't touch it."

"Then what would you do?"

"I'd go myself."

"You'd be stopped if you tried."

"I've been stopped once before." She remembered the event without pride. A man had been with her but he had faded away. It had all been handled extremely delicately. "I was going on an innocent holiday. They said I was stopped for my own protection."

"I don't remember you told me that."

"Why should I share a humiliation?"

"Next time it will be more than that."

"If there is a next time I'll plan it better."

He said again: "Don't do it, love."

She sat watching him with a warm affection. He was all things she had ever desired. In his time he had been an ardent lover; he was reliable and he gave her security; above all things he was a happy man.

Not, she unexpectedly thought – not in the least like Arthur Milden. She was astonished that she had thought of him: it must be the contrast with Dick. Yes, the contrast. Arthur had always been fighting something, more than half the time himself, and though he couldn't live without one he didn't really care for women. In Arthur Milden's ideal universe men would live on one side of the street, women on the other, apart; they would meet when their needs made a meeting imperative but otherwise go their separate ways, each of them speaking its peculiar language, each enjoying its particular interests. A civilisation still existed which pursued this ideal as far as it nowadays dared or was able but Arthur hadn't belonged to it and it was one which was threatening Judith's race.

She looked across at her husband again. He had finished his breakfast and had lit a cigar. He smoked three cigars a day and he smoked them deliberately. So there he sat in a solid contentment, throwing its comfortable aura round Judith, the woman he had taken to wife. Dull, you might think? She almost laughed. He had given her all that she wanted. She loved him.

He rose and turned on the morning news. Some pundit was talking on Mid-East affairs, talking of the occupied territories. Dick Maxe switched him off and returned to the table. He looked at his cigar. It burnt evenly.

"I wish they'd stop talking about occupied territories, it sounds like Belgium or Holland in the last war. In fact it is the other way round. It was you who were attacked by the Ay-rabs and in the process they lost a couple of provinces. If you care to keep them that seems perfectly reasonable."

"Plenty of people think violently otherwise."

"Plenty of people don't live in the country. Farming makes you respect realities."

His massive relaxation had eased her. "Such as culling an animal useless for breeding?" She had always wanted to bear him children.

"That's going to depend on the sort of animal. I've two old horses out at grass." He looked at her and smiled, unembarrassed. "Rather like myself," he added.

"You do talk terrible nonsense, sometimes."

"In that case let's leave it." He stubbed his cigar out neatly in a tray. His wife liked cigar smoke but not the stink of smouldering ends. "What are you doing this morning?"

"Not much. There's nothing actively cooking up."

"Good."

"But there's paperwork."

"Get a clerk to do it. If I know anything of the civil service you'll be grossly overstaffed with clerks. I beg their pardon. Clerical officers."

"Then what do you suggest?"

"A walk. I think I'll take a gun along with me. There's an old cock pheasant –"

"It's out of season."

He said with a mild but firm reproof: "As if I didn't know that. I do. But rules were made for fools, you know – the sort of people who shoot driven birds. Which I do not. Occasionally I shoot for the pot and I'll certainly shoot an old cock who's upsetting things. The culling you spoke of." He smiled. "Helping nature."

They returned two hours later, the dead cock dangling. Dick Maxe had stalked it and shot it sitting. As he'd said, he was a realist, not a man who shot birds in a senseless battue.

Judith watched him clean his gun with pleasure, the pleasure of watching a small thing done well. He knew what he was doing perfectly, his broad hands moved with an expert rhythm. When he had finished he put the gun aside. "Let's see what's on the box."

"All right."

It was a well-known Left Wing figure, frenetic . . . Israel must be brought to realise . . .

Dick Maxe snapped him off and said: "They're certainly making a meal of Israel."

"So will the Arabs if they get half a chance."

"You really think that that could happen?" He was suddenly, unaccustomedly formal. "I realise you know much more than I do."

She could recognise a serious question and was prepared to give a serious answer. "I can't be sure or not at the moment. That pot has come to the boil before without going over the top and into the fire. Nevertheless, as I said, I'm frightened. If things get worse –"

"You'd go to Israel?"

"If things get really bad I'd have to. I don't suppose you understand."

"Unhappily I understand perfectly. In your place I might do the same."

"You mean that?"

"To my shame I do."

"It's hard to believe."

"You don't have to believe it."

She rose and embraced him. "I love you dearly."

He was English and naked emotion embarrassed him. Instinctively he sought to cool it. "Then I think we've both of us earned a drink."

Normally he didn't drink before lunch but this morning he walked to the sideboard purposefully. He poured a Campari soda for Judith and a considerable brandy for himself. He held his glass up wryly and said:

"I'm going to miss you, dear Judith."

"I'm going to miss you wickedly too."

17

The Very Senior Legal Figure had asked Lord George to call at his office and Lord George had hidden a smile and gone. The position of Foreign Secretary was vastly more important and powerful than that occupied by the VSLF but in the formal pecking order was lower. In any case the VSLF was older than Lord George – much older. He had served in every Tory government since the mind of man ran not to the contrary, the Grand Old Man, the great survivor. He was distinctly shaky now and again but he still had a first class brain when he was not. Every prize he'd aimed at he'd gained but one.

Lord George was received with a certain stateliness, the manner that of the senior fellow receiving the junior lecturer kindly. "It was good of you to come," the old man said.

"Not at all. I am at your service. For the little I may be able to offer."

"Will you take a glass of Madeira wine? It is what I usually drink before luncheon."

Lord George knew this wasn't strictly true but it was part of the Senior Common Room act. The Keeper of the Royal Conscience rose, walking to a sideboard firmly, this morning surprisingly sure on his pins. He returned with two glasses of Madeira on a tray. Lord George, though he loathed Madeira, took one.

"Your very good health, sir."

"*Altrettanto.*"

Lord George looked round the room as the old man sipped. It was much as he had expected it would be – some fine old pieces clearly personal and photographs of young men at Cambridge, another of the VSLF in the uniform of the regiment he'd served in. He needn't have gone to the wars at all but characteristically had chosen to do so. Where he'd fought with some distinction and panache. Everything he had done he'd done well. Except for that single, still nagging failure.

Lord George wondered how long he'd take to come to the point. Men of his age and aura were not abrupt. He was astonished when the old man said crisply: "The Prime Minister is going to fall. That is, if he doesn't die first which seems probable."

Lord George was astonished but he was also respectful. This man had a greater experience than his own; he had seen five Prime Ministers come and depart and if he said Foxy was falling he probably was. Lord George decided to throw the ball back. "You've heard rumours about his health?" he asked.

"I'm inclined to believe they are more than rumours but I was thinking less of his health than his actions." The VSLF was suddenly, formidably formal. "I am addressing a fellow Privy Councillor?"

"Yes."

"Then the feeling which I sense around me, and I am not without a certain experience, is one of an increasing mistrust. There have been too many muddles and errors of judgement."

"If you're asking me I don't dissent but we don't want a general election now."

"There's no need for a general election whatever."

"Another backstairs knifing, then?"

"I deplore your choice of words but I understand. I asked you here to sound your intentions."

Lord George said at once: "I have no intentions. I suppose I'm just another meritocrat but as it happens I'm not all that ambitious. The price at the very top is too high."

"I think so now but I didn't once."

. . . And very near you were to it too. If you hadn't overplayed it grossly . . .

"May I ask if you'd run again yourself?" It was ironical and intended to be so but the shaft bounced off an old man's carapace. The VSLF said simply: "How could I? I happen to be a peer of the realm. A Prime Minister in the House of Lords is nowadays something quite unthinkable."

"Whereas I have a courtesy title of sorts but three brothers between myself and the real one? But the answer is still No. Emphatically."

"Will you take a glass of Madeira wine?"

"Thank you but I have had my ration."

The VSLF poured a glass for himself and Lord George used the time whilst he did so to think. He had noticed that the VSLF had shied quickly away from the Prime Minister's health but there might be a simple explanation of that: the old man knew. Not just rumours – *knew*. Foxy could have gone to him, telling the truth and asking for counsel. It would have been a perfectly natural thing to do. This Great Survivor had an unmatched experience, was the doyen of contemporary politics, and both of them had an interest in common. They didn't want the Hard Tories back. But if Foxy had offered a private confidence it would be bound by even tighter rules than the oath imposed on a Privy Councillor.

Lord George made a sudden guess and believed it right. Talk of an increasing mistrust was certainly true but also a smokescreen. Foxy was going to die and that was that. There'd be no night of the long knives nor need for it. But who succeeded Foxy was vital. The VSLF was making his soundings.

That was perfectly legitimate and Lord George himself had a personal interest. He decided to pick up the conversation at the point the VSLF had left it for more wine. "So I don't want the Prime Minister's job and you, for other reasons, are debarred. Who do you think it's going to be?"

"Would the others stand for Abbot, do you think?"

"Abbot is made of the finest putty."

"I must agree that Abbot is notably malleable."

It wasn't a word to be chosen at random and Lord George looked up at the old man sharply. No dribble of saliva flawed his chin. There was a suspicion of a dewlap there but the bone was as fine as ever, as thrusting. Above it two cool blue eyes met his own. This wasn't the man who dozed at meetings, waking to bore the assembly stiff with lectures on constitutional niceties or insistence that a British Riot Squad

142

would somehow offend the British conscience. It was a politician still close to the height of his powers.

He was asking now: "Would you serve under Abbot?"

"Yes, I would. He would leave me to get on with the job."

"The Chancellor of the Exchequer thinks the same."

. . . So he's talked to Ellis too. Be careful.

But need he be as careful as all that? This venerable but still potent figure could never reach the highest office but he was proposing that he become its grey eminence. On reflection Lord George was not offended. His distant ancestors had done the same, dancing the Georgian kings on strings whilst they themselves ran the country quietly.

The VSLF's next words confirmed this thought. "I haven't spoken to the Home Secretary yet but I'm confident he will feel the same."

So it was going to be a puppet Prime Minister. The real power with the Foreign Secretary, the Chancellor of the Exchequer and the Home Secretary. A triumvirate. Behind it this astonishing old man. It had worked before and very possibly would again; it might even win the next election which on the present omens looked hopelessly lost. In any case it was very much better than a return of the neo-Victorian theorists.

Lord George said simply: "I'm your man."

The VSLF relaxed at once. "I thank you. Then we can talk more freely. How do you stand on America?"

"Doubtfully."

"I do not trust her an inch myself." This Lord George knew – it was common knowledge. In his time as an eminent academic the VSLF had taught for a year at an Eastern and very Ivy League college. He had returned with a great respect for its scholarship and an equal contempt for American politics.

Which he was expressing now with a casual lucidity, casual because in his days as a student it hadn't been enough to be Alpha: you had to make the business look easy even if you stayed up all night polishing. "Vietnam was the classic example, I think. I don't mean going in – that was

143

justified – but they could have settled the affair in a week if they hadn't chosen to fight with one hand tied. So they come limping out after total defeat and the echoes of that still affect our daily lives." The old man drew breath but went on acidly. "You would think they would have learnt from that but they've just made the same mistake in the Middle East. One of their Congressmen put it admirably. 'If those Marines are there to fight they're too few. If they're there to be shot at they're far too many.' America could have set up and supported almost any of the factions it fancied but that would have meant a presence for a decade. Which the American people would not have accepted. Even a third-class man should have known that. But in he goes and out he comes again. He was always on to a beating to nothing."

Lord George had realised at once what was happening. The VSLF was doing the talking but this was in fact a *viva voce*, the sophisticated Oxbridge kind where the examiner threw out an idea and the candidate's rating depended on his reply.

"We can't afford to offend America but I wouldn't wish to become a vassal. It's a delicate balance and not easy to work with."

The old man nodded, clearly pleased; he asked with a sudden change of manner: "Do you read the *Daily Telegraph?*"

"No. I read the *Guardian*. I like a good laugh."

"Then you won't have seen this."

The VSLF fished in a drawer of his desk. From it he drew a newspaper cutting. He passed it over.

From Field Marshal Lord Eaglesfield, K.G.
Sir,

Recent correspondence in these columns appears, in my simple judgement, to miss a point. I am not qualified to comment on the moral or political aspects of stationing CRUISE in this country but on the military I may venture an opinion. There has been a great deal of talk about Dual Keys, but even if this arrangement existed does anybody seriously suppose that such a lock could not be broken?

It would be an irony if we were obliged to seek the aid of another Power to prevent the use of Cruise to our disadvantage.
Eaglesfield
Ascot, Berks.

Lord George handed the cutting back. "Very clear thinking indeed," he said.

"Contrary to the Left's mythology stupid men do not become Field Marshals. I knew Eaglesfield once but not as a Marshal. He was in fact my battalion commander and clearly marked to rise fast and far." The VSLF put the cutting away. He was waiting for comment and Lord George gave it.

"At the best I'm very lukewarm about CRUISE."

"I haven't made my mind up either but if the Opposition were not so shabby I might have written that letter myself. So there's only one other matter between us."

Lord George had been expecting it. "ANNE?" he enquired.

"Precisely. ANNE."

"Then besides a man's health you spoke of errors of judgement. In my view the way we're handling ANNE is a good deal worse than simple error."

"It's loyal of you to use the plural. I heard you oppose the plan in Cabinet."

"Trying to bargain ANNE for Trident – free? Not so much the plan itself – it was an outside chance and I suppose worth a try. What I bitterly opposed and still do is the decision to go for all or nothing. Short of Trident, I'd get a good price for ANNE. It would save the Americans time if nothing else. Plugging on as we are, this take it or leave it, ANNE is simply a wasting asset. The Americans will get it in time and we'll be left with no hand to play."

The VSLF thought this over deliberately. "And Russia?" he asked at length.

"Russia will get it too but not first. She has a superlative system of worldwide espionage which helps her to cut corners and save time. As it did over the original Bang. But she doesn't have the enormous resources and in a straightforward race will come in second."

145

"You seem very sure."

"I'm afraid I am."

The VSLF's sparkle suddenly faded; he looked tired and old, clinging on by a thread. "Afraid," he said, "is alas the right word. So three Powers will have ANNE and where does that take us? One step nearer to Armageddon. I'm the son of a High Church country parson. I escaped from all that in my last year at school but now as death creeps daily closer . . ." Unexpectedly he thumped the desk. "Damn the physicists and damn their nuclears. Damn ANNE as another work of the devil. I'm told that the thing is unstable."

"Very."

"Then I could hope that Yeldham goes up to heaven in the hell on earth it's designed to create."

Judith Maxe had been reading the newspapers carefully and what they had told her had increased an anxiety which had been sharpening over several weeks. For matters in Israel were going badly. The Lebanese adventure had failed since the PLO had miraculously escaped again and what had been left to take its place was no longer a hostile organisation sheltering in a state which resented it but a people which, torn as it was into savage factions, was united in a single emotion, a loathing and detestation of Israel. Moreover though the PLO's rump was now at a much safer distance individuals had been filtering back and there'd been another series of murderous outrages, two school buses bombed and settlements shelled. Three men had been captured and had claimed to be soldiers. Israel had promptly tried them as criminals.

It was incredible to Judith Maxe that opinion should exist which considered this wrong. But then Gentiles had incomprehensible values and notably less sense of co-hesion.

All this Judith Maxe's newspapers told her but her private sources had told her much more. There'd been the usual retaliatory airstrikes – Judith herself had often questioned their wisdom – but the losses had been much heavier than ever before. Missiles were no longer manned by peasants but by men who knew how to use their power and an attempt to take them out preemptively had failed and been disastrously expensive. The balance of power in the air had changed.

Judith's correspondent had been grim. If Israel's air force could no longer fly freely, blunting the edge of attacks as they came on, then come on they would with increasing momentum. No doubt they would take casualties, which was something they could afford and Israel could not, but they would know that they couldn't be stopped near a frontier in a single decisive battle which they'd lose. And once deep into Israeli territory any casualties would be insignificant, a small price for the extinction of Israel.

So they couldn't be stopped at a frontier, Judith thought. *They'd have to be*. ANNE would do that and do it decisively. The news had killed reason and conscious decision, older instincts had surfaced and gripped her helplessly.

She had had powerful help in making her plan and was surprised when it had fallen to pieces. They had chosen a derelict airfield in Norfolk, the buildings in ruins, the runways cracked. But they would take a light aircraft resolutely piloted and Judith who had been waiting quietly could hear one coming in in the darkness. It was showing no lights but she could make out its lines. She sighed and stepped away from the hangar and a man whom she hadn't heard or seen came out of its shadows and touched her arm.

"I'm afraid you can't do that," he said.

She stared at him, shocked and disappointed for she'd been told that she stood a very good chance. They'd also given her a two-two pistol but neither the knowledge nor will to use it. In any case it was now in her briefcase and the man had his eyes on that, not her face.

As if reading her thought he said politely: "And I've a colleague who's an excellent shot."

"Then what happens now?"

"We get rid of that aircraft."

He flashed his torch twice in the lightening darkness and two flashes came back in recognition. The light aircraft had halted, its engine idling, and a second man ran across to it quickly.

"I hope there won't be any unpleasantness." Judith's own

plan had now collapsed but she didn't want complications of any kind.

"Madam," the man at her side said stiffly, "if our information is right, and it mostly is, the pilot of that plane has protection. I dare say you know his country. So do we. But the last thing my masters would want on this earth is involvement in diplomatic hoo-ha. That plane will be turned round and will fly away. Alternatively there'll be a shoot out, in which case neither my colleague nor I will be given any sort of medal."

The second man had reached the aircraft and the pilot had opened the cockpit and leant out. They could hear two voices in altercation. One was angry, the other calm, and the calmer seemed to be winning the argument. After what seemed a long time but was not the hood of the cockpit was banged-to noisily. The pilot turned the light aircraft and flew away.

The second man joined the first. "That was lucky."

"Lucky my foot. Congratulations."

Judith Maxe interrupted peremptorily; she asked again: "So what happens now?"

"We have a car and will of course escort you."

"Escort me where?"

"That depends on the instructions I get when we stop at the nearest working telephone." They had reached the car and he opened the door for her. "In the back, if you please, and my friend will go with you. Your briefcase goes in the front with me."

When Charles Russell's telephone rang at five that morning he reached for it with a sense of foreboding. The caller wasted no time on compliments; he gave his name and named an airfield. "We have her," he said briefly and waited.

"An aircraft was picking her up?"

"It was."

"How did you handle that?"

"By the book. Since we didn't have specific instructions we played by the standing rules. Which are to avoid any diplomatic entanglement. We persuaded the pilot to fly away."

148

"No violence?"

"Argument yes, but violence no."

"You've done extremely well. And Mrs Maxe?"

"Is waiting in a car with my colleague."

"Luggage?"

"A briefcase. I suspect she's armed."

"But she didn't use it?"

"She hadn't time. If I'm right it's in that briefcase of hers. Would you like us to search it?"

"Certainly not. I doubt if it holds any secret documents – she could carry what she knows in her head – but if it did we'd be committed finally. We'd have lost any chance of papering this over."

"You are considering that?" The voice was astonished.

"I don't know yet, I need time to think. Meanwhile keep that briefcase out of her hands. I very much doubt that she'll shoot at you but I fear she might try to shoot herself."

ANNE, Russell was thinking, was notoriously unstable. At Yeldham it wasn't unique in that.

"Very good. And now?"

"You escort Mrs Judith Maxe back to Yeldham. Since I've met her and she knows what I do you may use my name when you give this message. Give her my sincerest compliments and tell her to keep inside that fence. If she comes out she'll be arrested. Openly. In which case I'll have lost my option. She's an intelligent woman who'll understand what I mean."

"Nothing more, then?"

"Not till I've thought."

Charles Russell got up and shaved and dressed miserably. It had been easy to talk of time to think but time guaranteed no solution whatever. He would summon his Board and consult it that morning and between them these wise old heads might deliver. But he himself could think of nothing. The dilemma was absolute. On the one hand another enormous spy scandal, on the other Judith Maxe, a traitress, indefinitely at large inside Yeldham. Of one thing he was entirely sure: he wouldn't take this story to Foxy. Foxy would pounce on the obvious solution, Foxy would point the finger at Judith. And this time Charles Russell would have no excuse. In the circumstances it would be a legitimate order. Judith wasn't Mr Arthur Milden and dealing with dangerous traitors was part of the job.

In the event the choice was not made by Charles Russell.

18

Next morning he read the report distastefully but also with the respect it deserved. It had been prepared in the Executive by a man who knew his business perfectly. It was lucid but it omitted nothing.

The first part, Russell decided, was not too bad. It dealt with Mr Arthur Milden and the position there was inescapable. No newspaper receiving a proof of that photograph (and the writer believed there'd be more than one) would publish as it stood without caption: on the contrary it would start burrowing fiercely and Azimev's identity was something which could be established easily. The fact that he'd been expelled for spying would be less easy to discover quickly, since neither the Russians themselves nor the Foreign Office was likely to be gladly co-operative; but the experienced journalist had tools today which his grandparents had never thought of and the expulsion would be unearthed within a week.

And then the cloudburst. What had a known spy been doing on a Minister's doorstep the night before he was due to be thrown out?

There'd be an instant flood of research into Milden and it wouldn't have to be very profound. Several reference books already recorded that Milden had once worked in Russia, where even the nosiest school of editors couldn't hope to send a man to discover the truth. That would have to be pleaded by Milden and Foxy, a perfectly innocent private friendship, and nobody would believe a word of it. There was going to be an appalling rumpus, the Opposition with its snout in the god-given trough.

Well, that was Foxy's business, not Russell's. He might ride it with his huge majority or conceivably they'd get him down. One thing he wouldn't do – go on grounds of health.

If he had to fall he'd take it standing. Russell had given his views on that: it wasn't his business, he wouldn't touch it. He certainly wouldn't arrange a killing to pull a dying Prime Minister out of a hole.

That was water over a suspect dam for which Russell was in no way responsible but there was another for which he surely was, the increasingly deadly battlefield which a word like "security" barely covered. And on this there'd been indecisive action. Judith Maxe had been stopped on the road to defection but the problem of her presence remained.

Charles Russell began to consider it, frowning. He could defend his action in stopping her leaving on a smallprint clause in her contract of service which said that she must ask permission before she tried to leave the country but no doubt there was also another clause which provided for termination of contract. She might invoke that and perhaps have it blocked but there was nothing to stop her requesting permission and if that were refused and she made the fact public there'd be an immediate storm of high-minded protest in the name of something called civil liberties.

And a bigger and for once justified uproar if it were known that she'd been confined to Yeldham. That instruction had been *ultra vires*; it had been bluff to buy time whilst they both of them thought and Judith, when she'd done so, might call the hand down.

The logic began to shape itself mercilessly. Judith's actions, unlike those of Milden, were within Charles Russell's accepted field. He had forgiven the Prime Minister a demand which he wouldn't have made if well, but he couldn't forgive himself in his lifetime if he failed in something he saw as a duty. In depressingly simple terms that was clear. It was to prevent Judith Maxe from betraying ANNE.

An accident in a car would be routine.

Or he could go down to Yeldham and talk it over. She was a reasonable woman as well as committed; she'd failed once with powerful help and would know she was watched. It was an outside chance but it ought to be taken.

No time like the present.

He made four telephone calls in increasing uneasiness. The first was to Judith's house. It rang out. The second was to the Establishment's switchboard. No answer. The third was to Milden. Again no answer. The fourth and final was to Milden's Ministry. There was a good deal of backing and filling here but finally Russell reached somebody senior. Who gave it to him straight as he'd asked it.

They'd been trying to raise Yeldham for half an hour.

Arthur Milden, like Russell, had been facing his difficulties and like Russell he'd had two, quite distinct. But unlike Russell he couldn't slough one of them by deciding that it wasn't his business. Peggy Milden emphatically *was* his business: he couldn't escape it by advancing disinterest. He had failed her all the way down the line. She was now on the streets to buy hard drugs.

He hadn't any doubt of that. Heroin had been found in her bag and when she'd run up the steps of his house to betray him, when she'd held his arm to set him up for the photograph, she'd had that daemonic fury he had seen once before, the desperation of the addict deprived. Withdrawal symptoms, he thought they called it. So they'd withheld her ration till she agreed to betray him. That black whom he'd just had time to notice sitting in the car which had brought her, inactive but entirely sinister. She had run back to him when she had played her part.

Milden felt little anger but great shame. Shame for what his daughter had come to and a greater shame that he'd allowed it to happen. He'd been altogether too soft and complaisant, playing for the occasional moment when she showed some sign of grudging affection, moments like the notable one when he'd spoken of his own bloodymindedness and she'd said there were times when she almost liked him.

No doubt there were all sorts of excuses. The devil's advocate woke and spoke for him. What *could* he have done when she wouldn't be helped, when all she wanted was steady money to live in the sleazy world she had chosen? Without motivation on Peggy's part her father had been entirely helpless. If he stopped her allowance she'd slide the quicker and he couldn't force her to take proper treatment if she didn't want to be cured – not in England.

Or more accurately he couldn't yet. The thought was the

worst of all, intolerable. She'd go down and down in her private hell before he could invoke the law or conceivably somebody else did it for him. By which time she would be incurable, a wreck of a woman, a burden for ever. He found himself thinking again, in fury, that there were things they did very much better in Russia.

He would see a good lawyer tomorrow but not in hope.

He turned to his second problem more coolly for it concerned himself alone and he wasn't ashamed. He had realised at once what that photograph meant, its implications for himself and for Foxy. One thing obviously – he'd ask for Milden's resignation the moment he saw the damning thing.

But would he confine his demands to resignation of office, Milden still in the House and able to state his case? He might ask him to resign his seat, even to go abroad for a while.

Arthur Milden was prepared to do neither.

It was five o'clock in the afternoon and Milden had decided one thing. He would spend the evening in steady drinking, then go to his bed and hope for sleep. His political career was in ruins, he had a daughter who was hooked on heroin. He looked like a successful man but his life had been one of unrelieved failure. If happiness were the end of life he'd have been happier as a middle-rank officer in that regiment which did its duty unquestioningly and shunned publicity like a vulgar plague.

He had taken the first of his planned evening of drinking when the telephone disturbed him peremptorily. He swore but picked it up reluctantly. If it were Peggy he'd put her off; he would have to do what he could to help her but he didn't want to do it this evening. But another voice said sharply: "Arthur?"

He recognised it as Judith Maxe's and he wished to speak to Judith Maxe even less than he wished to speak to his daughter. He hadn't spoken to her since taking Russell to Yeldham, conducting his daily business through his office. How did officials earn their keep but by acting as convenient buffers between yourself and an affaire which still rankled?

He said cautiously: "Yes. Arthur Milden here."

"Something has gone seriously wrong."

He was surprised that she should have bothered to ring him; he knew nothing of ANNE's esoteric mysteries but plain politeness demanded some show of interest. "Tell me," he said, "but make it simple. You know that I'm no sort of scientist."

"But you are an electrician."

"*What was that?*"

She said impatiently: "There's a dish in the oven and it's getting too hot. The worst we've ever had was One-Two-Four. At this moment it's One-Two-Nine and rising."

"Have you turned off the power?"

"Of course we have. But it seems to be out of control."

"Impossible." Apart from the elaborate switchgear there was a back-up system of fuses and cut-outs. He had designed them himself.

. . . He had designed them himself.

"Could your process generate heat of its own?"

"Not without breaking a dozen basic rules."

"Where are you now?"

"I'm in the laboratory. The others are all in the bunker."

"Join them."

A harsh laugh shook him as no words could have. "You seem to forget I'm the man in charge."

"I'll be with you in an hour."

"If I'm still here."

He had been doubtful about the electricity, such things didn't happen with modern lay-outs, but her "I'm the man in charge" had decided him. Yeldham was part of his botched-up Ministry. *He* was the man in charge. He'd have to go.

He drove to Yeldham fast but relaxed, not thinking in words like danger and duty, but conscious that the one existed and that the other was in his blood inescapably. You could cut your roots and sometimes miss them but you couldn't escape what came down by heredity.

At the gatehouse he had to ring twice and knock loudly before the gatekeeper came out in an overcoat. He normally wore a well-kept uniform and at once began to excuse his appearance. "I know we're supposed to be out of range – if anything goes wrong, I mean – but there's a cellar in this cottage and it's cold. My wife and I . . ." It tailed away.

"You were sensible. Now tell me what's happening."

"I only know it's a Red Alert. And they've called in the perimeter patrol. Normally they don't do that. I wouldn't go in, sir. I've rung the bunker."

"And what did the bunker tell you?"

"They're running scared. They've never called in the patrol before."

"So the guardhouse in the fence will be unmanned?"

"But the barrier down."

"A pity. I'll have to walk the last part."

"You really mean to go in, sir?"

"I must."

Milden motored on to the guardhouse annoyed, for if the bar were down he would lose several minutes. The bar was down and he noticed the counter-weight. He pushed hopefully upwards but it had locked automatically. He ducked under and began to run, remembering for no evident reason that although he had been quite good at games he hadn't been an athlete at school and therefore never of the school's élite. Now his unarmed combat had kept him fit but done nothing for his time over half a mile.

He paced himself carefully; he didn't wish to arrive in a breathless sweat. No soldiers came out of bushes to halt him, the siren was no longer blaring. Somewhere a blackbird, its instinct infallible, was sounding its alarm call stridently. Otherwise the silence was eerie.

He ran straight to the laboratory and at once lost his way in its maze of corridors. He called but nobody answered. He blundered on.

He turned a corner blindly, near panic, and suddenly he was there, the control room, the heart of this terrible place they called Yeldham. Judith was watching the bank of instruments. She turned as she heard him, said: "Ah, you came."

Her casual manner annoyed him further. "Of course I bloody came. What's happening?"

"The current is off but it's still coming through."

He crossed to a dial-face and read it. Zero.

"Where's the electrician?"

"Below."

"Then get him up here at once."

"Don't be silly."

"I order it," he said.

She laughed again, the same harsh laugh. "You can give me general instructions, you know – how much ANNE to make or rather to try to. But at Yeldham I'm the queen bee, not you."

Her manner was still pleasantly social and it left him defenceless and feeling futile. Anger or fear he might have coped with, a man against a frightened woman, but Judith was showing no sign of either. He said a little weakly: "Well?"

She pointed at the master dial briefly. "When I rang you that read One-Two-Nine. At the moment it's One-Three-Four and rising." She added coolly: "All records broken."

"God damn the records." He went back to the control panel angrily. The needle still pointed firmly at Zero. "I don't understand it."

"Nor did the electrician. He talked mumbo-jumbo about fuses and cut-outs –"

"Did he say they had blown?"

"He said they must have."

"That means precisely nothing."

"I know."

He tried to take her hand but she drew it away, looking at the watch on her wrist. "Dick gave me this," she said, "on our honeymoon. It still keeps good old fashioned time and gives the dates and the month if you happen to want them."

"Does it foretell the future?"

"Not quite."

"Then what's your own guess?"

She looked at the dial again: it had risen four points. "Maybe thirty seconds," she said.

In fact that was an overestimate.

EPILOGUE

The atoll had been scrupulously cleared of human life and even of animal before the scrap-iron ships had been anchored in clusters and the worn-out tanks exposed on its beaches. Now both were smouldering masses of metal, twisted into the shapes of nightmare.

Hair read the reports with satisfaction. There were one or two minor irritations, for instance those ungrateful islanders who'd been evacuated with absurd compensation to another and less infertile rock but were now clamouring that they'd been treated unjustly. They wanted to return – *with* their loot. Every Bleeding Heart in the western world had seized on their case and was running it strongly. But Hair could ride that and was ready to do so. He shared the opinion of one of his predecessors. The only thing to do with Bleeding Hearts was to stand aside and let them bleed to death.

But that apart the affair had gone admirably. Since the British had called it ANNE the name had stuck, and Hair's scientists had been pursuing her with all the ardour of their unmatched resources and the fact that no expense need be spared. Ten days ago they had thought they had her. The test on that atoll had proved them right.

Hair chuckled; he could afford to do so. No more chaffering with those awkward British who appeared to have made some slip at Yeldham which had destroyed the work of years in a second. As those tanks and ships had died on the atoll. The staff had been safe in a flameproof bunker but the physicist from whose womb ANNE had sprung was now part of a pile of stiffening ashes. No doubt there would be a formal inquiry – the British had a national compulsion for inquiries into matters better ignored – and afterwards they might try again. Or very possibly they would drop the whole project. ANNE was non-nuclear, that was part of her dowry, but British public opinion was not robust. As the news of her sheer horror grew there'd be plenty of people shouting for her death.

It didn't matter. Hair held her firmly and he held her alone. He hadn't needed the Service brass to explain to him what that meant strategically. So Russian massed armour comes pouring in and Russian massed armour is stopped in its tracks. Like that atoll again, like Yeldham but bigger. And not a nuclear fired, not a trace of fall-out. Russia would retaliate, demanding that ANNE be banned forthwith, taking out European cities to emphasise the demand wasn't bluff. That was something which Hair could bear with fortitude. They'd be European cities, not his own. There would be time to talk, to fix something up.

Europe was still a buffer state.